ERNEST J. GAINES

Catherine Carmier

Ernest J. Gaines was born on a plantation in Pointe Coupée Parish near New Roads, Louisiana, which is the Bayonne of all his fictional works. His novels include the much-acclaimed *The Autobiography of Miss Jane Pittman*, *Of Love and Dust*, *Bloodline*, and *A Gathering of Old Men*. He divides his time between San Francisco and the University of Southwestern Louisiana, in Lafayette, where he holds a visiting professorship in creative writing. His most recent novel is *A Lesson Before Dying*.

ALSO BY ERNEST J. GAINES

Catherine Carmier

Catherine Carmier

A NOVEL BY

ERNEST J. GAINES

VINTAGE CONTEMPORARIES

VINTAGE BOOKS

A DIVISION OF RANDOM HOUSE, INC.

NEW YORK

First Vintage Contemporaries Edition, April 1993

Library of Congress Cataloging-in-Publication Data
Gaines, Ernest J., 1933–
    Catherine Carmier: a novel / by Ernest J. Gaines. — 1st Vintage
    contemporaries ed.
        p.   cm. — (Vintage contemporaries)
    ISBN 0-679-73891-6
    I. Title.
PS3557.A355C36   1993
813'.54 — dc20   92-50589
CIP

Author photograph © 1983 Thomas Victor

Manufactured in the United States of America
10 9 8 7 6 5 4

Part One

CHAPTER ONE

Wᴴᴱɴ Brother got out of the car, the two Cajuns sitting on the porch turned to look at him.

"How y'all feel?" Brother said.

"Brother," the younger Cajun spoke in return.

The other Cajun smiled at Brother, but did not speak. After standing on the porch a moment, Brother went inside the store.

"Mail come?" he asked the clerk.

The clerk sat behind the counter, fanning himself with a piece of cardboard. He was a very big man with a red face and blue eyes. He did not answer when Brother spoke; he did not even look his way. Brother stood in front of the counter, wondering whether he should ask him again.

"Mr. Claude?"

The clerk waved the piece of cardboard before his face, but he was sweating as if he stood out in the sun bare-headed. Two old black fans in the ceiling spun slowly and monotonously, but they seemed to make the place warmer instead of cooling it off. Brother passed the tip of his tongue over his dry lips.

"Mr. Claude?"

"Goddamnit," Claude said, looking at Brother. "Why the hell can't y'all come out here the same

3

time? Look like the hotter it get the more you niggers want to bother people."

He threw his fan to the side and went to the mailbox at the end of the counter. The mailbox was one of those wooden boxes used on office desks for incoming and outgoing papers. The clerk cursed again before gathering up the mail.

"You want it all?" he asked, without looking around.

"Yes, sir," Brother said. "Checks, too, if they done come."

The clerk turned from the mailbox, threw the mail on the counter, and went back to his chair to sit down. After looking at each letter, and then putting them all in his pocket, Brother dropped some money on the counter and got a bottle of cold drink out of the icebox in back. Claude looked at the bottle in his hand when he passed by the counter, going onto the porch.

"Pissed off in there, hanh?" the older Cajun asked Brother.

"Reckon'd so," Brother said.

"This heat," the Cajun said.

"Guess so."

"Don't pay him no mind," the Cajun said. "This heat. Cussed out me and Paul the same way."

"Yeah," Paul said. "I say, 'How it go there, Claude?' He say, 'Cram it up your ass.'" The Cajun smiled. "This here heat, there."

They were silent awhile. Brother drank from his cold drink and looked at the river on the other side of the road. The river was very calm and blue. The trees on the other side of the river looked black, and Brother noticed a car, quite small from this distance, passing through the trees.

"See you not working today?" François, the older of the two Cajuns, asked Brother.

"On vacation," Brother said. "Three weeks."

"Yeah?" François said, looking up at Brother from his seat on the floor. "I thought y'all get your vacation in the winter there?"

"Taking mine now," Brother said. "My friend coming in from California."

"Yeah?" François said, squinting up at Brother. "Oh, yeah, yeah, I hear 'em talk 'bout him there in the field. That boy there Charlotte, no?"

"That's the one."

"Yeah, I hear 'em talk 'bout him there," François said. "So he come visit the people, hanh?"

"Might be to stay," Brother said. "From all I done heard 'bout it."

"Stay?" François said. "People leaving here; not coming back."

"That's what I heard," Brother said.

"And what he do here?" François said. "Farming? It's all gone."

"Think he go'n teach," Brother said. "Think that's what he studied for."

"Yeah?" François said, looking up at Brother from under his sweat-stained straw hat. He wanted Brother to say more, but Brother did not.

Brother drank from his bottle and looked out at the river. Two motorboats raced by the store, going toward Bayonne. Brother watched the boats until they were out of sight, and drank from his bottle again.

"How's the work going?" he asked François.

He wanted to change the conversation from his friend to something else. Maybe he had already said too much about Jackson. White people were suspicious and afraid of strange Negroes; and they were more suspicious and more afraid if they knew that those Negroes came from the North.

"All right," François said.

"Taking the day off, huh?"

"Waiting for that tractor," the other Cajun said.

"Y'all getting another one?" Brother asked.

"Yeah. Everybody got one now."

"Reckon'd you can destroy some land with all of 'em going," Brother said.

"Yeah," François said. "Knock it all out in one day like that."

Brother drank the last of his cold drink and took the bottle back inside the store. The clerk behind the counter was too busy fanning himself to look at Brother when he came into the store or went back out.

"See y'all," Brother said to François and Paul. "Hope your tractor hurry up and get here."

"Thanks," Paul said.

Brother got into the car and backed away from the store. The two Cajuns watched him turn around and go back up the road. He did not have to go far, and François could see him turn down the dirt road and park the car in the ditch.

"You think he one of them people?" François asked Paul.

"Who?" Paul said.

"Them things there. You know. Them demonstrate people there."

Paul shrugged his shoulders and leaned back against the wall. Paul wore khakis, a pair of brogans, and an old sweat-stained straw hat. He cocked his straw hat over his eyes and looked out at the river. François could tell that Paul did not care who Brother's friend was or what he did.

CHAPTER TWO

Brother parked the car in the ditch and turned all the windows down. If there was any wind stirring at all, he would be sure to get it.

When he sat up again, he saw another car coming his way. It was Raoul Carmier's car, and Catherine Carmier was driving. Catherine was driving slowly, but the car still spread dust on either side of the road. She blew the horn as she went past Charlotte Moses's house, and Brother thought he heard Charlotte speaking to her. A moment later Catherine had driven up to where Brother was and had parked the car in the ditch across from him.

"See you just relaxing yourself?" she said.

"Waiting for somebody," Brother said.

"Come out here to meet somebody myself," she said. "Oh, but it's hot today."

"Burning up," Brother agreed with her.

Catherine opened the door, then she took off her straw hat and began fanning with it. Brother looked at Catherine, but each time she looked in his direction, he turned his head away.

Catherine Carmier was Negro, but with extremely light skin. With her thin lips and aquiline nose, with her high cheekbones, dark eyes, and dark hair, Catherine Carmier could have easily passed as an Indian.

The Carmiers lived in a large old house about three hundred yards from the highway. The house had once belonged to the white overseer, but when the Grovers, who owned the plantation, began sharecropping, the overseer and his family moved away. No other white man wanted the house, and since the Grovers refused to rent it to a Negro, the house remained vacant.

One summer afternoon, Robert Carmier rode up to the plantation store (the store was still being managed by the Grovers then) and asked Mack Grover for the house. (Antoine Richard, who was at the store, brought this version of the story into the quarters.) "What color are you?" Mack Grover wanted to know. "I'm a colored man," Robert Carmier said, "but I can farm as well as the next one." Mack Grover told him that he had a smaller house farther down the quarters that he would let him have. Robert Carmier repeated that he could farm as well as any man and better than most. Mack

Grover told him that the other house farther down the quarters was smaller and would be easier to keep up. Robert Carmier told him that he would keep up this one as well as anyone kept his.

Antoine Richard said there was silence after this, and he lowered his head to look at the floor. He saw a grain of rice at the foot of the counter and began moving it with the toe of his shoe. He moved it out, then in, from one side to the other; and still neither one of them said another word. He raised his head and looked at them again. First, the colored man—tall, slim, whose hair was as black as a crow's wing; who held his hat in his hand. Hat in hand, yes, but not fidgeting with it one bit—as any other Negro would have done, and many whites, too, who stood before Mack Grover—but holding it as steady as a professional beggar would hold his. Only Robert Carmier was not begging. The eyes said this from the moment he came into the store until he walked out. He had come up there as a man would come up to a man, and he had asked for the house as a man should ask for a house. He had taken off the hat, not because he, Robert Carmier, thought he should take it off, but because someone in the past had told him that this was the proper thing to do when asking a favor.

Antoine Richard looked at the other one next. Mack Grover was one of the landowners, not the only one, but the one responsible for hiring or discharging. He was considered the best of the Grovers by the Negroes, the worst Grover by the whites. He was forty-five or forty-six, still a bachelor, and both winter and summer he could be seen in a seersucker suit. Every morning he stuck a match stem in his mouth, took it out at mealtime, then put it back again. Now as Grover stood there contemplating Robert Carmier, Antoine Richard found himself not looking at either man, but at the white speck of sulfur on the end of the match stem. He knew that when the match stem moved to the other corner of Mack Grover's mouth, he would give his answer.

"Will day after tomorrow be too early?" Robert asked.

"What?" Mack Grover said, as though he were surprised that Robert would dare open his mouth before he was given orders to do so.

There was silence again. The swarm of flies that had been flying around in the sunlight all afternoon darted into the shadows. Antoine Richard thought they were gone for good this time, but before you could count to three, they were back again. A truck went by the store, then a bus went by and blew, but neither Mack Grover nor Robert Carmier seemed to be conscious of anything but each other.

Antoine Richard saw the match stem move halfway and stop, then go on.

"Friday," Mack Grover said, and turned away.

"Wednesday would be much better for me," Robert said. "Especially since it's already empty."

Mack Grover turned again, but not completely around.

"Wednesday, huh?"

They looked at each other only a moment this

time, then Robert made a slight nod, put on his hat, and went out. Mack Grover and Antoine Richard followed him onto the porch and watched him ride away on the horse.

"You know him?" Mack Grover asked.

"Heard o' him," Antoine Richard said.

"Well?"

"Good worker from what I hear."

Mack Grover and Antoine Richard watched the horse move farther and farther away from the store.

"I'm going to regret this," Mack Grover said. "I'm going to regret this sure."

"He'll car' his share," Antoine Richard said. "I know 'bout them kind o' people."

"His share of the work, yeah," Mack Grover said. "But that ain't enough for a nigger, no matter how white he is."

CHAPTER THREE

A hard rain fell all day Thursday and most of Thursday night, and when Robert Carmier tried to cross the bridge on Friday to come into his yard, the bridge broke into halves, and the wagon went into the ditch. Robert told everyone on the wagon to get off, the furniture would be carried the rest of the way by hand. Besides Robert there were three others: his son Raoul, his wife Lavonia, and his sister Rosanna. The Carmier family was much larger than this (there were five daughters and one son altogether) but the girls had all gotten married and left. Two of the daughters, who had once lived in Opelousas, were now living in Bayonne about fifteen miles away.

Two men from farther down the quarters stopped by the wagon and asked Robert if he wanted help. Robert thanked the men very politely, but told them that their help would not be needed. A light drizzle had begun to fall again, and the men stood under the oak tree by the fence and watched the people carry the furniture into the yard. For three or four hours that afternoon, the two men and two women moved from the wagon to the house. By now a crowd had gathered under the tree to watch them. No one left until the last piece of furniture had been taken inside, the wagon had been pulled out of the ditch, and the bridge fixed again.

It was soon learned in the quarters that the Carmiers had little use for dark-skin people. They went by without speaking, and when you spoke to them they hardly nodded their heads. When they needed help to get in their crops, they hired people their color. Once the work was done, the people left, and no one saw them until the crops were ready to be harvested again.

Robert Carmier and his family made as much crop for Mack Grover as any family that size could make. Morning until night, six days a week, they were in the field. Then every Sunday morning, they got into the buggy and went to the Catholic church in Bayonne. Around five in the afternoon they would return, change into everyday clothes, and sit

out on the porch. They visited no one, and no one
in the quarters would dare visit them. Every so
often one of the daughters would come in from
Bayonne or New Orleans, but the rest of the time,
Robert and his family, the four of them, would be
seen on the porch alone.

One day Robert and one of the Cajun share-
croppers got into a fight. It was winter, and both
men were hauling their cane to the derrick. They
were about a quarter of a mile apart when they saw
each other. Each man started whipping his team,
each trying to get to the derrick before the other.
Robert got there first by only a few feet, and the
Cajun, so angry that he had lost, ran his team into
the back of Robert's wagon.

"What the hell you trying to do?" Robert
hollered at him.

The Cajun leaped from his wagon onto Robert's
wagon, pulling Robert to the ground. When Mack
Grover and several other men broke up the fight,
both Robert and the Cajun were bloody.

"I'll send you to hell for this," the Cajun said to
Robert. "I'll send you to hell for this for sure."

"You come, you come in front," Robert said.
"You can bring the whole goddamn family, just
come in front."

"Well, nobody's going to hell long's I'm here,"
Mack Grover said. "Robert, get on that wagon."

About three months later, Robert disappeared.
No one knew how, nor where to. That morning he
had gotten on his horse and left for Bayonne. Neither he nor the horse was ever seen again.

A few days after Robert's strange disappearance, the two women moved across the field to another house. No one in the quarters knew exactly why the women had gone, but every other person had an opinion. One was that the house was haunted—Robert's ghost had been seen several times by several different persons; another was that Raoul was courting a woman that neither his mother nor his aunt approved of; still another was that the woman he was courting did not like the mother nor the aunt.

When Della Johnson came to the house, everyone brushed aside the idea that Della could dislike anyone. Not only did she love her in-laws whom she visited across the field, but she had a nice word to say to anyone else who went by the house. She would stand on the porch or out in the garden, talking to you so long that you would have to say, "Della, I just have to be getting home. I've spent more than my time already." And even after you had said that, she would find something else to talk about to keep you there a few minutes longer.

One day while going to the store, Olive Jarreau stopped under the big oak tree just outside the fence and called for Della to come to the window. Della did not answer. Olive called again—she called at least a half-dozen times—but Della never did show up. Olive knew she was in there, because she had heard Della singing just as she came up even with the house. That same afternoon, Sue Jacks spoke to Della in the garden. Della mumbled something under her breath, but that was all. Sue Jacks had a few minutes to spare, but Della did not. Sue Jacks went on, thinking little about it, because even a person like Della would have "off days" at times. But Aunt Rose Culluns did not feel as Sue Jacks did when she spoke to Della and Della pretended she did not hear her. Aunt Rose fussed all the way to the store and all the way back down the quarters again. "Well, he got her jest like he want her," she grumbled to herself. "She couldn't stay that way for long, not around something like that."

CHAPTER FOUR

There were three children. They were Catherine, Mark, and Lillian. One day when Catherine was six years old, she came home from school and told Della that she had a boyfriend.

"Oh?" Della said, smiling. Then Catherine noticed how quickly the smile left her face. "What color he is, baby?"

"He's dark."

"Dark? How dark?"

"Well," Catherine said, going from one finger to another; "he's darker than me, he's darker than you, he's darker than Daddy, and he's darker than Marky. Mommy, can he come play with me sometime?"

"Yes," Della said. "But he'll have to leave before Daddy gets home, you hear?"

"Yes."

"And that's going to be a secret between us, you hear? Just me and you, you hear?"

"Yes, ma'am."

The second child was Mark. Everyone knew that the second child was not Raoul's. He was darker than anyone else in the family, and the children at school were always teasing him about it. One day while Raoul and the boy were sawing down a tree in the woods, the tree suddenly made a false turn, crushing the boy into the ground. The people in the quarters called it murder, but the sheriff, as well as Mack Grover, agreed with Raoul that it was an accident. After this happened, Della was seldom seen any more. The people saw her go into the field and come back home. Whenever she was at the house she remained inside. Catherine did all of the outside work.

The third child was Lillian. She was less than a month old when she was taken to New Orleans by one of Raoul's sisters to be brought up as a lady. It was Lillian whom Catherine had now come to the highway to meet.

CHAPTER FIVE

The bus stopped. Brother watched two people come down the aisle and step to the ground. Then as the bus pulled away, he heard Catherine whisper, "Jackson?"

The two people came across the highway. Brother recognized the girl immediately. She was Lillian, Catherine's sister. But was the man really Jackson? Jackson was only a boy when he left here. This man was six feet tall or better.

"Jackson?" Catherine whispered again. "Yes," she said. "Yes, it is."

She threw her straw hat back into the car, and she tried to fix her hair, straighten her dress, and pass her hands over her face before he saw her. She started toward Jackson and her sister, then stopped, and waited for them to come into the quarters. Brother did not move either. What could he say? Anyhow, this might not be Jackson at all. There was something too different about him—something Brother could not put his finger on at the moment.

When they came into the quarters, Lillian saw Catherine and came over to where she was. Jackson followed her with the two suitcases. Lillian and Catherine embraced, and Lillian kissed Catherine very hard and long. Then as she stepped back to introduce Catherine, she saw that Catherine and Jackson were already looking at each other.

"Catherine," he said.

She bowed slightly, smiled, but did not say anything. It was obvious to everyone that she was too filled with emotion to speak at that moment.

"I can tell you two already know each other," Lillian said.

"Yes," Jackson said. "How've you been?" he said to Catherine.

"Fine."

Neither one of them said anything else, but they continued looking at each other as though there was much more to talk about between them. Then suddenly Jackson seemed to catch himself; he smiled embarrassedly and looked away.

"Stranger," Brother said, coming up behind him. Brother had been standing by the car looking at Jackson and the two girls. He had not come up to him before, because he was still not sure that it was Jackson; and besides that he had very little to say to either one of the girls. He spoke to them when he met them in the road, but that was as far as their conversation went.

"Brother?" Jackson said.

"That's me," Brother said, smiling and nodding.

Jackson set the suitcases on the ground and grasped Brother's hand.

"Damnit, man, you done growed some there," Brother said. "I wouldn't 'a' knowed you."

"You look the same."

"Yeah, me, I never grow," Brother said, laughing. But the laugh ended almost as quickly as it had begun. There was something about Jackson's face that made him feel that his laughing was out of place. A moment of silence followed. Neither one of them could think of anything more to say. Brother smiled uncomfortably and lowered his eyes.

"Well, I think we'll go on down," Lillian said. "Thanks again for taking my suitcase off for me."

"It was nothing," Jackson said, turning to her and glancing at Catherine. "Why don't we go over to the store and have a cold drink? I can stand one."

Lillian glanced at Catherine quickly and shrugged one of her shoulders. "All right with me," she said.

"Miss Charlotte got lemonade at the house," Brother said, moving in closer.

"That's better still," Jackson said. "We won't have to buy it."

There was a look of apprehension on both Catherine's and Lillian's faces.

"Maybe some other time," Catherine said.

"Afraid I might bite you?"

"No," she said. "But I have to go up the road to get the mail."

She and Jackson continued to look at each other and Jackson seemed to understand what she meant. He nodded his head.

"Maybe some other time."

Lillian, who had turned away unnoticed, was staring out at the river. Jackson put her suitcase in the car, then came back to get his own. He looked at Catherine and nodded again. She was trying to tell him something with her eyes, which he seemed to understand quite well. He and Brother got into the car and drove away.

"I said that 'cause I knowed they wouldn't go," Brother said.

"And I shouldn't get too close, huh?"

"Left to her she would 'a' gone," Brother said. "Left to her, she 'ud do lotta things. But it's Raoul."

"He's still the same?"

"He go'n die the same."

"Nobody has taken her from him yet?"

"And nobody go'n do it."

Jackson did not say any more. He looked out of the window, but seemed only half interested in the things they were passing.

CHAPTER SIX

Charlotte was getting ready to go out on the front porch for about the tenth time that afternoon when she heard her back gate slam shut. She had an idea who it was, and she turned around in the door and came back into the kitchen. A young woman, wearing a big yellow straw hat and a white dress, came up to the door and knocked.

"It's open," Charlotte said. "Just get in 'fore them flies do. They waiting."

The girl looked tired, but managed a smile as she came into the kitchen. Two strings of perspiration ran down her face.

"Look how you sweating," Charlotte said. "Bet you run all the way from the Yard."

"Yes'm."

"Eh, Lord," Charlotte said. "Fall in one of them holes and break your leg there, hear."

"I'm careful most the times," Mary Louise said.

"If you know like I know you better be careful all the time," Charlotte said. "I don't see how come they don't chop them weeds down."

"Reckoned they waiting for the frost to kill 'em," Mary Louise said.

"That's probably the only way they'll get down," Charlotte said.

Mary Louise smiled and looked toward the front door.

"You'll hear it come 'round Morgan Bend," Charlotte said. "It ain't failed to blow in thirty years."

"Truck blowed there few minutes ago and I thought that was it," Mary Louise said. "Ought to been seen me running out to the front."

"Can't you tell a truck horn from a bus horn?" Charlotte said.

"Most the times," Mary Louise said.

"I can tell that horn in my sleep," Charlotte said.

But she had gone out there also when she heard the horn blow. It was still too early for the bus to show up, but when one is as anxious to see another person as she was to see her nephew (he was her grand-nephew, her niece's son) time does not matter. "That's it, that's it," she had said, running out on the porch. Then as the big oil truck went past the road, Charlotte looked both left and right to see if anyone had seen what she had done. She did not see anyone, and she moved back inside, but stood just behind the screen. "Should 'a' knowed it was too early," she said. "I'm just's jumpy's a flea."

Then they heard it—two great blasts. Their

hearts leaped into their throats. They looked toward
the door, then at each other. Charlotte nodded her
head; Mary Louise smiled.

Then suddenly Charlotte spun around. Mary
Louise thought she was going out on the porch, and
Mary Louise started after her. But Charlotte turned
toward the dresser to check herself in the mirror.
First, the kerchief. The kerchief was all right. The
dress. She pulled it one way, then the other, then the
same way again. She found a speck of lint on her
shoulder and brushed it off, then she brushed off the
other shoulder for safekeeping. Then she brushed
off the front of the dress, each side, and turned
around and brushed off the back. She faced the
mirror again, and this time she did not like the way
the kerchief fit her head. She tried pulling it into
shape, but finally took it off and stuffed it into a
drawer.

She turned from the dresser to look over the
room again. The floors had been scrubbed that
morning, the walls and furniture dusted several
times since, but still she felt that something might
have been missed. She went from her room into the
room where he would stay, then back into her
room, and finally into the kitchen. She raised the lid
off one pot to look at the gumbo, then the lid off
another pot to look at the rice. She got a dishtowel
and began waving it at three houseflies that swarmed
around in the sunlight. The flies darted in all
directions, and though she was an expert at getting
them out of the kitchen or knocking them down on
the floor and crushing them under the sole of her

shoe, this time she was unable to get even one. She hung up the towel and came back into the front again.

"Well, I guess that's it," she said. "I thought you would 'a' been out there."

"No'm," Mary Louise said, shaking her head.

She had wanted very much to go outside and watch the bus stop in front of the quarters. But she had told herself that it would not have been fair to Miss Charlotte for her, Mary Louise, to be the first one to see him get off.

CHAPTER SEVEN

They stood on tiptoes to look at the bus. When the bus drove away, they saw two people coming across the highway.

"That's him?" Charlotte asked.

"Must be," Mary Louise said.

"Look like he got somebody with him," Charlotte said. "Look like she white."

"Yes'm," Mary Louise said. "She look white from here."

"Lord—don't say that," Charlotte said. "Don't tell me Jackson done done something like that."

Mary Louise did not say anything. She was both afraid and jealous of the other woman. She moved to the end of the porch and held onto a post to get a better look. She saw the woman who looked white going toward the car where Catherine stood.

"I think that's Lillian," Mary Louise said.

"Lillian? Who Lillian?" Charlotte said.

"Catherine sister," Mary Louise said.

"Thank heavens," Charlotte said. "Thank the good Lord. What they doing, talking?"

"Yes'm, I believe so. Yes'm, that's Lillian. Her and Catherine just hugged. And I can see Brother. He talking to Jackson, and now they shaking hand. That's Lillian."

"Thank the Lord," Charlotte said. She passed her hand over her forehead because she had suddenly begun to perspire. "You can't tell what might get into children head these days."

Mary Louise came from the end of the porch to stand beside Charlotte. Charlotte tried to see what was going on at the front, but could not, and she asked Mary Louise to look again.

"Just talking," she said.

"Still talking to Raoul gals?" Charlotte asked.

"Yes'm."

"That just's bad's white," Charlotte said. "Worser. They still talking?"

"I think they getting ready to come now," Mary Louise said.

Charlotte began rubbing her hands together. What was she going to say when she saw Jackson? What was she going to do? It had been ten years since she saw him—ten long years. And now he was coming back.

How should she meet him? Where? The gate? In

the road? Wait for him to come up to the house? Where?

"They coming," Mary Louise said.

Charlotte's heart beat faster. Her mouth began twitching uncontrollably. A heavy lump rose up in her throat, and her legs became weak.

No, she thought. Please; please don't y'all fail me now. Able me to stand. Able me to see him first.

The car stopped, sending a cloud of dust all over the place. Charlotte did not know when she left the porch, how she went down the steps or through the gate. She threw her arms around Jackson, almost knocking him back inside the car. She laid her head against his chest, and there for the next few moments she prayed and wept.

She raised her head to look at him again. Brother stood at the back of the car with the suitcase. Mary Louise stood in front, looking at them.

"Stand back," Charlotte said to Jackson. "Stand back."

She stood away instead, and looked at him, and nodded her head.

"Yes," she said. "Yes."

Then she went up to him again and kissed him hard on the mouth.

"Yes," she said; "I prayed. And, yes, He sent you back."

"How've you been, Aunt Charlotte?" Jackson asked, looking down at her.

Brother, standing at the back of the car with the suitcase, saw a thin smile come on Jackson's face. That's it, Brother thought. That's what I seen out there. He just won't let go.

"Little sick there in the grinding," Charlotte said. "But I can't feel no better 'an I do right now."

"You look well," Jackson said, looking down at her as though he wanted to say more, but something inside of him kept him from doing so. He looked at the girl who stood to the side.

"Isn't that Mary Louise?" he said.

"Course that's who that is," Charlotte said. "Don't tell me you done forgot Mary Louise now?"

"She has changed," he said. "How are you?"

"All right," she said, smiling.

"Been waiting like the dickens," Brother said.

"All right, Brother," Mary Louise said.

Brother laughed. Jackson looked toward the house. It was a small gray house with two doors facing the road. A line of hedges that needed cutting badly stood just inside of the picket fence, and a small mulberry tree to the left of the house threw its shadow across the yard and part of the porch. Jackson looked at all of this before going into the yard. Everything—his aunt, the house, the trees, the fence—seemed strange, and yet very familiar.

"Let's go in," Charlotte said; "you can get out that coat."

CHAPTER EIGHT

When Jackson came out on the porch again, Brother and Mary Louise were sitting in the swing, and Charlotte sat in a rocker in the middle of the porch. Another chair was next to her chair. The chair had not been there before Jackson went inside.

"Come here and sit down, Jackson," Charlotte said.

He sat in the chair beside her.

"It's you, ain't it, Jackson? Ain't it? I ain't seeing things, is um?"

He smiled his thin smile. "It's me, Aunt Charlotte."

"I been praying so much, hoping so much I might see you and you ain't even here."

She took his hand and rubbed it, then she touched the side of his face and his chin. She had to touch him, to feel him, to make sure that this all was not a dream. She nodded her head.

"Yes," she said. "Yes. It's you. He wouldn't fool a old servant—not that bad."

Jackson let her hold his hand, but he would have felt better if she did not. He loved her—he probably loved her more than he did anyone or anything else, but scenes like this one embarrassed him.

"How did you leave your mon?"

"She was well."

"Still got that one bad boy?"

"Only one. Yes," he said.

"Ain't talking 'bout coming out here?"

"No," he said.

"I guess when they leave, they forget the old place. Just like they forget the old people."

Jackson did not say anything, and Charlotte continued holding his hand and looking at him. Every few moments she would give the hand several little pats on the knuckles. This hand that she remembered so well assured her that he was there.

"But you never?"

"No. I never forgot," he said.

"No, you couldn't," she said. "Not you. Not you. Now you finished?"

"Yes," he said.

"And you can go right on to teaching?"

He made a frown and started not to answer this, but he thought better of it and agreed with her.

"Y'all hear that?" Charlotte said. "Y'all hear? Now he can teach."

She was talking to Brother and Mary Louise, but she was looking at Jackson all the time.

"That's learning for you," she said. "That's learning for you. That's going—keeping going. Yes, that's what that is."

She squeezed his hand and smiled up at him. She did not know whether she liked that little beard and that little mustache that was trying to break out in his face. She had never thought of him as having a beard or a mustache. She had thought he would look the same as he did when he left her. Maybe a little taller, but that would be all. But in spite of these things—even the way that his voice had changed—she had never felt so proud as she did at that moment.

"The same place," he said.

"Up here," Charlotte said. "But if you go farther down there, lot of the houses done been tored down. All where they was, now you got crop. Cajuns cropping all the land now."

"The Cajuns?" Jackson said, looking at her.

"Yes. They done just about taken over this old plantation now. When Mr. Mack died, that was it for the colored people. Mr. Bud there, all he do is drink. Ain't worth a penny."

"Aren't there any colored farmers at all?" Jackson said, pulling his hand free. He did it so casually that Charlotte did not notice him. Or if she did, she must have felt that he preferred it being free.

"Raoul the only colored one now," she said. "All the others done gived up. Spec' the only reason he ain't, he just so stubborn. But they won't be contented till they taken his just like they did all the rest."

"How do they take the land when it's not theirs?" Jackson asked.

"They got they way," Charlotte said. "A white man'll find a way to take something, that's for sure."

"What are the people doing now?"

"Plenty of 'em done moved away," Charlotte said. "Some of 'em work for the Cajuns. Some of

'em just work out. Brother there, he working for
Three Star now."

Jackson looked over his shoulder at Brother
sitting in the swing. Brother nodded his head and
smiled.

"Yeah; waiting on tables," he said.

"And Mary Louise taken my place when I quit
the Yard," Charlotte said. "Her and her pa live over
there now."

The house Charlotte mentioned was a small
cottage that had turned a dust gray from so much
rough weather. A cow cropped at the short grass in
the yard. A white-faced calf was trying to suck
from the cow, but each time he got set, the cow
moved up again. On the other side of the house, a
sugar-cane field came all the way up to the yard.
Jackson remembered when this was not a field at all,
but a place where he used to play baseball.

"They took our ballpark, too?"

"They got it all," Charlotte said. "All but what
Raoul got."

Jackson looked across the road and farther down
the quarters at the big, old unpainted house where
the Carmiers lived. He could hardly see the house
for the trees in the yard, but the house looked no
different from the way he left it ten years ago.
Regardless of how bright the sun was shining, the
big trees in the yard always kept the yard and the
house in semidarkness.

There have been some changes, Jackson thought,
and there haven't been any. The Cajuns have taken
over the land and some of the people have gone

away, but the ones who are left are the same as they ever were. Just as that house and those trees were and will always be.

"Jackson?" Mary Louise said. She was standing beside the chair with a pitcher of lemonade and three glasses. Jackson took one of the glasses and she filled it for him.

"Thanks very much."

"Miss Charlotte?"

"That's not for me," Charlotte said.

Mary Louise went to the swing and poured a glassful of lemonade for Brother, then took the pitcher back into the kitchen.

"Having a little supper for you tonight," Charlotte said. "Nothing big. Just something, though. People down the quarters probably show up."

"You shouldn't have gone to the trouble, Aunt Charlotte."

"Wasn't no trouble on my part," Charlotte said. "They the ones wanted you to have it."

"No trouble on mine, neither," Brother said. "All I done was got the stuff and brought it here. Miss Charlotte and Mary Louise done the work."

Jackson nodded his head and drank from the glass again. When he was through, Mary Louise took the empty glass back into the kitchen.

"You look a little tired," Charlotte said to Jackson.

"I am," he said. "Traveling almost three days."

"Maybe you ought to get yourself little rest 'fore the supper tonight."

"That might not be a bad idea," Jackson said. He

excused himself and went inside the house.

"And I better get to getting myself," Brother said; "and take the rest of these people they checks. Don't need nothing else right now, huh, Miss Charlotte?"

"No, not now," Charlotte said. "But remember, you s'pose to come up here early tonight."

"Don't have a thing in the world to do," Brother said, "but take this here mail down the quarters. That won't take me mo' 'an a minute or two."

"Anytime 'fore dark," Charlotte said. "Tell 'em all down there I say howdy."

"Yes'm," Brother said. "Check you later, Miss Charlotte."

"What was that?" Charlotte said.

"I mean I'll see you after while," Brother said.

"I done told you 'bout that 'checking me,'" Charlotte said. "One of these days you go'n find something bouncing off that little steeple head of yours there."

Brother laughed and went down the steps. After getting into the car, he blew the horn at Charlotte and drove off.

"You see, that boy still playing with me there," Charlotte said. "You watch, I'm go'n surprise him yet." But as she watched the car go down the road spreading dust across the field, she shook her head and smiled to herself. "Eh, Lord, children, children, children," she said. "It take all kind to make this world go 'round."

CHAPTER NINE

When Mary Louise came out on the porch again, she stood by the door fanning herself with her straw hat.

"Jackson went in?"

"Yes. To rest up a while."

"Ought to be getting on back to the Yard, myself," Mary Louise said. Mary Louise naturally talked slowly—dragging out each word as though it took effort on her part to do so—and with the heat as intense as it was today, she seemed to be talking even more slowly than usual.

"You don't have much more to do, huh?" Charlotte asked.

"Take in the clothes; iron 'em tomorrow."

"Maybe I can give you a hand sometime tomorrow."

"No, thanks, Miss Charlotte," she said, waving the straw hat before her face. "I can do that little work."

She heard the car leaving the highway, and she turned her head to the left to watch it come down the quarters. Catherine was driving slowly, and as she came up even with the house she blew the horn and waved at Charlotte and Mary Louise on the porch. Both of them waved back at her. Lillian, sitting in the front seat with Catherine, did not turn her head.

"How them two can be sisters, I don't know," Charlotte said.

"Hear she going up North," Mary Louise said, dragging out the words as slowly as she moved the straw hat before her face. "Reckoned it's to pass."

"Wouldn't doubt it a bit," Charlotte said.

They were silent a minute, both watching the car go down the quarters and then turning into the gate.

"Well, I better be getting on back over there," Mary Louise said, but still not moving.

"Can't spare another couple minutes, huh?" Charlotte asked her.

"Yes, ma'am," Mary Louise said. "Something you want me do for you, Miss Charlotte?"

"Just sit here with me a minute."

Mary Louise sat in the chair that Jackson had been sitting in earlier. Charlotte did not say anything to her. Instead, she looked at the little mulberry tree at the end of the porch. The tree was covered with dust from the roots up to the leaves.

Mary Louise sat fanning herself very slowly. She realized that she should be getting back to her work, since she had promised them that she would only be gone a couple of minutes. But Miss Charlotte had something to say, and she would not leave until Miss Charlotte had spoken. She just would have to make up a good excuse for them when she got back.

"What you think of him?" Charlotte said. "He the same to you?"

"I don't know, Miss Charlotte."

Charlotte looked at her now. The eyes that were

happy only a moment ago were now thoughtful, questioning.

"The truth. I want the truth," she said.

"I don't know," Mary Louise said. "He just getting here."

"But he don't act like the same.person?"

"He been gone a long time."

"You still love him?" Charlotte asked.

Mary Louise nodded. "Yes, ma'am."

"And Catherine?"

Mary Louise looked toward the big, old house farther down the quarters. She did not answer Charlotte.

"You think he still love you?"

"I don't know," Mary Louise said.

Charlotte looked at the girl who was like a daughter to her. When she was sick in the winter and could not get out of bed, it was Mary Louise who spent as much time at the house waiting on her as she did at her own house.

But like a daughter, and only like a daughter, did she love the girl. She had never thought of her as being her daughter-in-law. She had sacrificed too much of her life to educate him to let anyone take him from her. Now that he was back, there would be no one but the two of them.

But she wanted to know if Mary Louise had seen something in Jackson that she might have missed. How did Jackson feel about her? about the place? Most of the young men and women his age were leaving the country for the city. Did Jackson feel the same way? Would he prefer teaching in Baton

Rouge or New Orleans to Bayonne? Baton Rouge would have been all right; he could come home every weekend. But New Orleans was too far away to see him as much as she wanted to. Charlotte searched Mary Louise's face for the answer. Mary Louise fanned very slowly with her straw hat, apparently deep in thought.

"Well," Charlotte said, "we'll talk about it some more."

"Yes, ma'am, I better get on back over there," Mary Louise said, as though it took all of her strength to bring out the words. She tied the big yellow straw hat on her head and stood up. "I'll see you after while, Miss Charlotte."

"All right," Charlotte said.

Mary Louise went back inside to pass through the kitchen, leaving Charlotte sitting out on the porch alone. Charlotte looked up and down the road, then at the swing, and at the chair beside her. No one was anywhere in sight; no birds sang in any of the trees; no dogs barked anywhere in the quarters. . . . The grave is something like this, Charlotte thought; something just like this. Just 'while ago, they was all there, and now they all gone. The grave is something like this. . . . But do me, Lord, here I'm thinking 'bout graves and all that and he just getting back here. Eh, Lord, they beg and beg for You to send they children back, and soon as You does, instead of they getting down on they knees and thanking You, they start thinking 'bout graves. Let me get on in this house and kneel myself down on that floor, yeah.

And while she knelt beside her bed with her hands clasped together, he lay across his bed in the other room wondering when he would tell her that he had come here only for a visit and would be leaving within the next few weeks.

CHAPTER TEN

When Brother drove away, Catherine and Lillian got into the other car.

"Want to go up the road?" Catherine asked.

"Don't we have to go for the mail?" Lillian said sarcastically.

Catherine did not answer her and drove out onto the highway. Lillian sat back in the seat, looking at her sister.

"How well do you know him?" she asked Catherine.

"Fairly well," Catherine said.

"I never saw him before," Lillian said.

"He left before you started coming back—ten, eleven years ago."

"I can tell by the way he talks he's not from around here—from the way he acts, too. Did he ever come to the house?"

"Sometimes."

"You mean when Daddy wasn't there?"

"Yes," Catherine said.

"Didn't Mama mind?"

"Mama loved him like he was her own."

Lillian continued looking at Catherine.

"Did you ever go over to their place?"

"No," Catherine said wearily.

"I don't suppose I have to ask why."

"I wasn't supposed to," Catherine said.

"He wasn't supposed to come there either, but he came."

Catherine smiled and nodded thoughtfully. "Yes, and paid for it when he got back home."

Lillian looked at Catherine, waiting for her to go on.

"Miss Charlotte used to almost kill him any time she found out," Catherine said.

"I didn't know she was like that, too."

"She's like that, all right," Catherine said.

"You all seem to get along so well—you and her. You're always speaking to each other."

"That's different," Catherine said. "Speaking across the fence is different from being at each other's house."

"Then she's no better than Daddy?"

"I never compare them, Lily," Catherine said. "I never judge them. They're the way they are."

"I suppose he had forgotten all about that when he asked us to go over there," Lillian said, looking at Catherine. Catherine remained silent. "And maybe he didn't think it was still going on. I'm afraid he has a lot to learn—an awful lot to learn about home."

Lillian looked out at the river which ran along the highway. The river, blue, serene, level as a mirror one moment, was suddenly disturbed by two motorboats racing toward Bayonne. In each boat was a boy and a girl waving and shouting at those in the other boat. Lillian watched the boats cut through the water as they went behind a clump of willows that grew along the riverbank.

"The idle rich," she said. "The idle white rich. Do they still fish out there?"

"Some," Catherine said. "But they use it mostly now for racing—stuff like that."

"They won't even let the poor fish in peace," Lillian said.

"That's about the size of it."

"That's right," Lillian said. "We must always remember it's theirs to do what they want with it."

After the car had passed the trees, Lillian could see the boats again. She stared grimly at them as they went farther away from Catherine and her in the car. One moment she wished she was there in the boat, the next moment she hated the mere sight of them on the water.

"How are they?" she asked after a while.

"All right."

"In the field, I suppose?" she said, still looking out at the river.

"Yes."

Lillian turned to Catherine, and already her face had become red with anger.

"What are they doing out there, Catherine?"

"They have weeds out there, Lily."

"Weeds?" Lillian said.

"Lily, please don't come back acting like that this time," Catherine said. "Please. Please don't."

"How should I act, Catherine?"

"I don't know, Lillian. If you don't know, I don't know, either. But you only come home twice a year, and every time you do, you're acting the same way."

"I should be jolly—jumping up and down—is that how I should be?"

"That might be better for everybody. I'm sure Mama would rather see you like that than moping 'round the place all the time."

"Catherine," Lillian said, leaning toward her, "Catherine, listen to me. Daddy's world is over with. That farming out there—one man trying to buck against that whole family of Cajuns—is outdated. Can't you see that? Can't you understand that? It's the same thing his sisters are trying to prove in the city. Can't you see that?"

"You'll never understand, Lillian."

"I understand, all right," Lillian said, and sat back in the seat. "Only I admit it. I admit it and you won't."

They were coming up to the post office, and Catherine did not say any more. She parked the car by the steps and went inside to ask about mail. The door of the post office was open, and Lillian could look inside the small one-room building at her sister talking to the clerk behind the screen. She saw Catherine turning away empty-handed. Catherine came back outside and got into the car.

"The mail?" Lillian said.

"It's gone."

"We knew it all the time, didn't we?"

Catherine was silent.

"Didn't we, Catherine?"

"I couldn't tell him I couldn't go over there."

"Won't he find it out?"

"He'll understand."

CHAPTER ELEVEN

After picking up the mail at the store, Catherine drove into the quarters. As she came up to Charlotte Moses's house, she looked for Jackson on the porch. He was not there. Catherine blew the horn and waved at Charlotte and Mary Louise, and both of them waved back at her.

"I see he's not there," Lillian said.

"I didn't know you looked."

"I didn't have to," Lillian said. "I just looked at your face."

Catherine smiled to herself and glanced through the rearview mirror to see whether Jackson would come out on the porch. He did not. After driving about two hundred yards farther into the quarters, she drove onto a small bridge and stopped before a gate. Lillian got out to open the gate for her.

"Want to ride up to the house?" she asked Lillian.

"I'll walk," Lillian said.

Lillian shut the gate and stood by the fence, looking over the yard and at the house. A half-dozen or more trees—pecan and oak—went from the fence to the house, from front to back. Gray Spanish moss hung from most of the trees all the way to the ground. The yard was covered with dead leaves.

The house, big, old, paintless, sat on wooden blocks at least three feet high. Eight or nine wooden steps led up to a long and warped front porch. A chair was propped behind one of the doors and a cat had climbed into the chair and gone to sleep. Lillian felt so depressed from just looking at the place that she asked herself how would she ever spend the summer here.

"When was the last time you killed a snake?" she asked, coming toward Catherine.

Catherine had parked the car under the shade in back, and she had come around the house with the suitcase. She held the suitcase in both hands, waiting for Lillian at the end of the porch.

"Just yesterday," she said. "Caught him going under the house. Frisky little rascal."

"Should have been exciting," Lillian said, looking over the yard.

"Missed him the first couple times," Catherine said. "But I got him. Scroochy little old thing."

"Scroochy?" Lillian said.

"Well, you know; wig-wagging, moving fast."

Lillian looked across the yard at the cornfield that came up to the back fence. But the mere sight of the field, the odor of the hay and dry corn, seemed to make it hotter—depressing her even more.

They went up onto the porch. The old porch creaked as they walked across it to the door. The cat in the chair looked up at them but would not move. Catherine picked him up and dropped him on the floor. The cat stretched himself, yawned, and rubbed against the leg of the chair.

"Where's Nelson?" Lillian asked.

"I took him over on the lane this morning," Catherine said. "Auntie and them kept him. I'll go back and get him after supper tonight."

They went inside the house and down a dark narrow hall to Lillian's room. The expression that came on her face when she entered the room showed that she disapproved of everything in the room, including the curtains that hung at the window. Catherine set the suitcase beside the bed and turned to her again.

"You're going to change now, or do you want something cold to drink?"

"I better get out of these things," Lillian said. "I'm about to burn up. How are they—Auntie and Grandmon?"

"All right," Catherine said. "Grandmon isn't getting around at all any more. Auntie does everything over there now."

"I might go over there with you tonight."

"They said for you to be sure to come."

"I might go—I'm not promising anything. It's

burning up, isn't it?"

"I suppose it was hot like this in New Orleans," Catherine said.

"No, it was not," Lillian said. "This is the hottest place in the world."

After changing into a more comfortable dress, Lillian followed Catherine into the kitchen. The kitchen was big and spacious with all sizes of pots and pans hanging on nails against the wall. The floor had been scrubbed that day and crushed red bricks had been sprinkled over it. In the corner by the window was a white gas stove, and across from it, by the door that led up the hall, was a big modern refrigerator. The kitchen table, which had been handmade, but well done, sat in the middle of the floor, facing the back door.

Catherine opened the window and went to the refrigerator to get the cold drinks. After looking over the kitchen with the same disdainful look that she had given her own bedroom, Lillian sat down at the table. When the cat came up to her and rubbed against her leg, she picked him up to hold in her lap.

"A piece of cake?" Catherine asked.

"Yes, I am a little hungry," Lillian said.

Catherine cut off a piece of cake for each one of them and brought the things to the table. Lillian set the cat on the floor and began eating. When Catherine sat down, Lillian looked across the table at her.

"How've you been, Cathy?" she asked.

"I've been all right."

Lillian did not like the way Catherine looked. Catherine looked tired. She was only three years older than Lillian, but she looked much older than her age. The clothes she wore, the way she talked and carried herself, all gave you the impression of a much older person.

"When did you hear from Bernard?"

"Quite a while now."

"He quit writing?"

"Yes."

"Isn't there anybody, Cathy?"

"No."

"There ought to be."

"I'm happy."

"Really, Cathy?"

Catherine ate slowly, trying not to look at Lillian. Lillian continued to stare at her.

"I love my sister, that's why I talk to her like I do," Lillian said. "There ought to be somebody."

"I have my child."

"Is that enough, Cathy?"

"I know what you're getting to, Lily," Catherine said, looking at her now. "My answer is still the same. I'm going to stay here with them."

"If it means to throw away your life? Not only yours, but your child's too?"

"I don't think I'm throwing away my life. I'm doing what anybody would do."

"Not anybody."

"Well, I'm doing what I think is best."

Lillian held the fork in her hand, looking across

the table at Catherine. She had eaten only a small piece of the cake. She had not touched the bottle of cold drink.

"Catherine, what's wrong with this house?"

Catherine looked at her and broke off a small piece of cake.

"Nothing," she said.

"What's wrong here, Catherine?" Lillian asked as though she had not heard her.

"Nothing," Catherine repeated.

Lillian frowned impatiently, looking across the table at Catherine.

"I've been asking this ever since I started coming back here, and you keep saying nothing."

"There is nothing."

"Then why don't you leave?"

Catherine looked at her.

"Go the way you're going, Lily?"

"Go any way you want to."

"No thanks, Lily."

The two sisters looked at each other, then Catherine looked away.

"You don't like what I'm doing?"

"You're grown, Lily. You can do what you want to."

"But you don't like it?"

Catherine was silent.

"Maybe I ought to marry somebody black and bring him here to meet Daddy. That would be just nice, wouldn't it?"

Catherine remained silent.

"Only I can't marry anybody black. I can't look

at a black person with anything like that in my mind. They've made sure of that."

"All you want is an argument, Lily—you don't care what about."

"I want answers."

"I've given you all the answers I know."

"You've given me a bunch of lies, Catherine, but no answers."

Catherine looked at her and looked away again.

"You're all I have, Catherine," Lillian said. "If you don't give me the answers, who will?"

"You have a mother and a father, Lillian."

"By name only."

"They're real."

"They're strangers to me. They're more than strangers to me. They're two people I can't stand to be alone with."

"Have you ever tried?" Catherine asked.

"Don't put that blame on me, Catherine," Lillian said. "Don't shift it on my back now. I didn't walk out of this house—remember that. I was taken away from here—sent away from here—traded off like a dog."

"Nobody traded you off. You was put there to get an education."

"I got one. A thorough one. One on hating."

"They didn't tell you to hate, Lillian," Catherine said.

"Didn't they? Everything black. My mother is not black, but she was thrown in as an extra subject."

"Don't say things like that, Lily."

"Why not, Catherine?"

"Because they never told you to hate Mama. I'm sure they didn't."

"Not directly—no. Because then I'd want to know why. But indirectly they told me a million times to hate her. There're so many little ways to make you hate, and they used every one of them." She stopped and looked at Catherine a moment. "That's why I say you're the only person I have. Those in the city, Mama and Daddy, they're all strangers to me. There's a fence between us. I can see them, I can hear them, but I can't feel them. I can feel you. You're the only person I can feel. . . .

"That other way—I've thought about it. I've thought about it over and over. I'm not in love with it. I can't ever be. But I have no other choice. I'm not black, Cathy. I hate black. I hate black worse than the whites hate it. I have black friends, but only at a distance. I feel for my mother, but only at a distance. I don't let my black friends come close to me. I don't let her come close to me. I don't say get away. I've never said that. I just can't open my heart out to them.

"I haven't opened my heart out to that white world either. But I'm going there because I must go somewhere. I can't stand in the middle of the road any longer. Neither can you, and neither can you let Nelson. Daddy and his sisters can't understand this. They want us to be Creoles. Creoles. What a joke. Today you're one way or the other; you're white or you're black. There is no in-between."

Catherine remained silent. She was not looking at Lillian, but she was listening.

"This is the last time I'll be coming here, Catherine. When I leave this time, I'm leaving for good. I want you to understand why. I don't care if the others do or not. I don't give a damn—"

Catherine looked at her painfully.

"No, Catherine, I don't give a damn. Mama—I really don't hate her. It's just that I can't get up any close feeling for her. I want to—yes; but I can't. As for the others, I don't care if they live or die tomorrow—that includes Daddy." She was silent a moment. "I want to say everything. I want to clear up everything this time. I don't want any kind of questions to stand between my sister and myself— the only person that I can, probably ever will, love."

Catherine continued to look down at the table and not at Lillian.

"I want you to understand, Cathy. I want you to understand what has happened to us, and what is still happening. You to understand, Cathy. Only you."

Catherine raised her head slowly and looked at Lillian.

"Do you understand, Cathy?"

She did understand, but she did not say anything. What could she say? She did not approve of what Lillian was doing. But she did not have any other suggestion.

Lillian looked at Catherine and turned away. Catherine's hand touched Lillian gently on the arm.

Lillian looked at her again, but she did not find in Catherine's face what she expected to see there. She wanted approval, she found love.

"What do you want for supper?"

Lillian shook her head. "I don't care."

"A chicken'll be all right?"

Lillian nodded her head. "If that's what the others want."

Catherine squeezed Lillian's arm a little. Lillian looked at Catherine and felt like crying. But this would have been a sign of weakness. She could not afford this.

CHAPTER TWELVE

Catherine had finished cooking, had taken a bath, and put on another dress when she heard the tractor coming out of the field. The sun was nearly down, throwing the shadows of the house and the trees across the road. The dust in the road, which had been stirred around all day by people going up and down the quarters, was now trying to settle. And the chanting of crickets and croaking of frogs had begun to fill the air.

Catherine came into the kitchen where Lillian sat reading a book. Catherine was wearing a pink dress with a little white collar and short sleeves. Raoul had bought the dress for her about a month ago, but this was the first time that she had worn it.

"What are you reading?" Catherine asked.

"One of those romantic novels," Lillian said.

"Love and all that?"

"And fighting and robbing. A little of everything." Lillian looked at the dress. "I like your dress," she said.

Catherine was wearing it especially for Lillian, because Lillian was always complaining that she did not have anything decent to wear. She turned around so Lillian could see the dress both front and back. Lillian smiled, nodded, and went back to reading her book.

Catherine could hear the tractor more clearly now. She knew it had crossed the railroad tracks and had come into the quarters. She stood by the table looking down at Lillian reading the book. She knew that Lillian heard the tractor, too.

"Lily?" she said.

"Yes?" Lillian said, not looking up. Lillian seemed to know what Catherine had in mind.

"Why don't you open the gate?"

Lillian shook her head and continued reading.

Catherine stood over her a moment and went out into the yard. She arrived at the gate only seconds before the tractor did. She had just unchained it and swung it open when Raoul drove across the bridge. Catherine shut the gate and followed the tractor to the back. It was dark now and she could hardly see Della climbing down from the trailer to the ground.

"How did it go?" she asked, coming up to the trailer.

"All right," Della said.

Della took off her straw hat and the head scarf that she wore under the hat. Catherine could smell the sour sweat-dirt odor of the scarf.

"Been hot all day," Della said.

"Murder," Catherine said.

Della looked at Catherine in the dark. She looked at her long and questioningly. Catherine knew the meaning of this look, and she nodded her head.

Della looked toward the house. The light in the kitchen was on, and Della could see the light shining through the door on the ground.

"What's she saying?"

"Same thing."

"Still leaving?"

"Still leaving."

Della nodded slightly, as though this was what she had expected to hear.

"Maybe that's the best," she said. "Maybe it is. I don't know."

"Hey, up there," Catherine called to Raoul.

Raoul sat upon the tractor racing the motor. He did not hear Catherine, and Catherine yelled at him again. He still did not hear her.

"What did you cook?" Della asked.

"A chicken," Catherine said.

"Good," Della said. "I'm just 's hungry 's I'm tired."

"Did you get through?"

"Couple rows left. Can knock that out in half a day."

They went across the yard toward the house.

Della stopped at the water faucet to pass some water over her face. Catherine knew she would wash up again when she got inside, but she was doing this now before meeting Lillian. She looked at Catherine for approval. Catherine nodded. They walked on. When they came inside, Lillian raised her head long enough to smile, to say, "Mama"; then she looked into the book again.

"Lillian," Della said.

And for the moment, those two words were the limit of their conversation.

"Fix me some water, Catherine," Della said.

Catherine half filled the washpan with hot water from a kettle on the stove; then she drew in some cold water from the faucet in the wall and carried the pan to the window. Della laid her head scarf and her straw hat on top of the refrigerator and went to the window to wash. There was silence: Lillian with her head down in her book; Della washing her face and arms as quietly as possible; and Catherine standing back looking at both of them. She heard the tractor motor turned off, and Raoul walking toward the house. Raoul was about to say something to her when he saw Lillian sitting at the table. Raoul stopped so suddenly that you would have thought he had come upon a stranger in his house.

"Daddy," she said.

Raoul nodded and passed Catherine the crocker sack that he had brought from the tractor.

"What's in it?" Catherine asked. "Last time, I put my hand on a half-dead 'coon."

"Mushmelons," Raoul said.

CHAPTER THIRTEEN

Supper was eaten in near silence. Della asked questions every now and then, but Lillian's answers were so dry and abrupt that Della would be silent several minutes before saying anything else. Lillian kept her head down throughout the meal. Everyone at the table could see how uncomfortable she was, and this made everyone else feel uncomfortable also. Catherine asked Raoul questions about the field, but his answers were as dry and abrupt as Lillian's answers were to Della.

"And we can finish it out tomorrow?" Catherine said to Della.

"In a couple hours," Della said. "Got no more than three or four rows. I can do it myself before twelve."

"That's the last piece, huh?" Catherine asked Raoul.

"That's it," Raoul said, without raising his head.

"Well, I'm glad of that," Catherine said. "That cotton'll be ready in a few weeks."

"Afraid we still got a while, yet," Della said. "A month at the least."

She looked across the table at Lillian. Lillian picked a small piece of chicken off the plate and put it in her mouth. Della watched her chew it slowly.

"I guess y'all don't get too much fresh chicken in

New Orleans?" Della asked, trying to start a conversation.

"No, ma'am," Lillian said, without looking at her.

"Well, we got plenty of 'em 'round here," Della said. "Any time you want one, just let somebody know."

Lillian chewed her food slowly and did not say any more. When she was through eating, she nodded her head—to no one in particular, but to everyone at the same time—and went out of the kitchen.

"What I ever done to deserve this?" Della said. "What?"

"You sent her there," Raoul said. "What you expect?"

"I didn't send her," Della said, looking at Raoul. "Eighteen years—but I'll never forget that. I didn't send her. Your people, they took her. But I didn't send her. I don't believe in sending children from home like they little dogs or something."

"Well, no use crying over spilt milk," Raoul said.

"And what I'm supposed to do?" Della said. "My own child won't speak to me—you tell me what I'm supposed to do."

Raoul went to the stove to pour a cup of coffee, and did not sit at the table again. When he had finished drinking his coffee, he unhooked the lantern from against the wall and went out into the yard.

"Don't cry over spilt milk," Della said. "We haven't spent an hour together all the time she been coming back here, but I'm not supposed to cry over spilt milk. God—what I'm supposed to do? What? Just forget her?"

Catherine started to say something, but she did not know what to say. She turned from the table and looked out of the door.

"Why'd they have to do it? Didn't they hate me enough themself? Why did they have to make her hate me, too?"

"She doesn't hate you, Mama."

"She doesn't? When she won't look at me—you don't call that hate?"

Catherine was silent. Then she turned to Della. "Mama, let me tell her. Let me tell her and get this over with."

"And what then?" Della said. She was crying. "What then?"

"That's the chance we'll have to take," Catherine said.

"The chance? Suppose she hate me more? What will she think of him? She hate him enough now. What will she think of him then?"

"We have to do something, Mama. You and Lily can't go on like this the rest of your life."

"I rather it be this way than worse."

"How can it be worse than it is now?"

Della was silent. She looked down at the table, crying softly to herself.

"I don't ever want you to tell her. No. Because if you told her about him, then you'll have to tell her how he died." She looked at Catherine a moment. "How you going to do that?"

"I'll tell her it was an accident. It was an accident."

"Will she believe it? Will the world let her believe it?"

"Mama, Lily is grown up enough now to understand."

"Is she, Catherine? How, when they never gave her the chance?"

"I still think that's the best thing to do."

"No," Della said, shaking her head. "I don't ever want you to tell her that."

"This can clear up everything, Mama, don't you understand? It can make her see what they've been doing to her. This might change Lillian's entire life."

"It might," Della said. "It might not." She looked at Catherine again. "If I didn't love your father, Catherine, I couldn't 'a' put up with this all my life. He don't know it, and if I told him, he wouldn't believe me. But I love him, I love him. And I wouldn't do anything in the world to hurt him—nothing. I'd blame myself if Lillian didn't see it the way we do—if she looked at it the way the people in the quarters do. Don't you see it's for him? It's for him."

Catherine did not say anything, and she turned to look out of the door. Raoul went past the door with the lantern. Catherine saw the shadows of the fence post and water barrel move jerkily in the direction opposite to Raoul's. After a while she stood up and began clearing the dishes off the table. She carried them to the big dishpan on the shelf in the window. She was nearly through with the dishes when she thought about Jackson again. She looked over her shoulder at Della.

"Guess who came back today?" she said.

Della raised her head and looked at her. Her face showed that she had no idea.

"Jackson," Catherine said.

At first the name did not ring a bell with Della. Then she recognized it, remembered him, and Catherine could see the smile coming on her face.

"Our little Jackson?"

"He's not so little any more," Catherine said. "He has a mustache now."

"Well, done Jesus," Della said. "Ain't that's something? I bet you Charlotte's tickled to death up there."

"I suppose so," Catherine said. She could see how happy Della was to hear about it.

"Yes, indeed," Della said. "I'm so glad for her." (And for a moment, she thought how she would feel if her son could come back to her. But that moment passed away like a puff of smoke.) "Did he bring a wife with him? He ought to be old enough?"

"No. He didn't bring anybody."

The smile began to leave just as it had approached—slowly. Catherine saw it and saw the meaning of it and turned away.

"Catherine?" Della said.

"Yes?"

Della waited for her to turn around; she did not.

"Turn around," Della said.

Catherine did, but she would not look at Della. "I see," Della said. "I see." Catherine turned away again. "Don't you be the one now," Della said. "Don't you be the one to hurt him."

And as Della said this, Catherine saw Raoul go across the yard with the lantern again.

CHAPTER FOURTEEN

The people started coming up to the house around sundown, and by eight o'clock the house, the porch, and the yard were filled.

Brother, who was in charge of seeing that everything went all right, was all over the place. First you saw him in the kitchen, then the living room, then out on the porch, and finally in the yard. Then back on the porch, the living room, and the kitchen again. Whenever he came into the kitchen, he got himself a bottle of beer out of the washtub near the door, uncapped the bottle on an opener on the wall, and stood there a moment drinking and looking around. Standing there now, he watched Charlotte and Mary Louise dish up food for an old man called Dude Claiborne. Charlotte dished up the rice and passed the plate to Mary Louise. After pouring a cupful of gumbo over the rice, Mary Louise passed the plate on to Dude.

"Ahhh," he said; "looked good, now it smells good. Aiii, but it's hot."

"Better sit down, Dude," Charlotte said.

"Yes," he said, going to the table. "Aiii, but it's hot."

"Something to go with that, Mr. Dude?" Brother said.

"One of them oranges if you got one," Dude said.

Two tubs were on the floor by the door. The one on the left had soft drinks, the other one had beer. Brother got an orange drink out of the tub on the left, uncapped the bottle, and set it on the table.

"Thanks," Dude said, bowing his gray head several times. It was obvious that he did not get this kind of attention often. He dipped up a spoonful of gumbo and rice and ate it noisily. "This good, Charl," he said.

"Thank you," Charlotte said.

"Yes," Dude said.

Brother moved back to the door and looked at Charlotte and Mary Louise again. Charlotte and Mary Louise had begun serving two other people. Brother thought everything looked all right in the kitchen, and he went back into the living room. He did not care for the living room; the living room was too noisy. Babies were crying, children were chasing one another around chairs and under the bed, and the women were too busy talking to pay attention to either. But Brother felt that since Charlotte had given him the job of keeping order that night, he had to spend as much time in the living room as in any other place. After standing in the room only a minute or two and reprimanding one little boy for jumping on the bed, he went out on the porch. Here, the boys and girls were sitting in the swing and along the railing of the porch. Brother did not want to eavesdrop on whatever they were talking about, and he went out into the yard. The men were out there, both old and young alike.

"Thinking 'bout Baton Rouge," a young man was saying.

"You been thinking 'bout Baton Rouge ever since y'all quit farming," an older man said.

"I'm thinking 'bout it se'ious now, though," the young man said.

"And what you go'n do in Baton Rouge?" the old one said.

"Do something," the younger one said. "Ain't doing nothing but starving here."

The men were silent a moment. Everyone seemed to be reflecting on what the young man had just said.

"Wouldn't 'a' thought ten years ago the Cajuns would 'a' been running things now," another, short, stocky, fellow said after a while.

"It been coming," someone else said.

"It ain't just coming. It here now," the young man said. "The only thing you can do is get away."

"Easy to say. But where you go? What you do? Where can a man go with a houseful of children?"

"Should 'a' kept your dick in your pants," someone else said. The men laughed a moment, then they were silent—reflecting the fate the Cajuns and their machines had bestowed upon them and their children.

Brother moved away from the crowd, and after looking over the rest of the yard and the porch, he went back inside the house. Charlotte saw him come into the kitchen to get another bottle of beer.

"You better eat something," she said. "That beer on a empty stomach go'n make you sick."

"Eat when Jackson get up," Brother said.

"Jackson ain't up yet?" Charlotte asked.

"No'm."

"Go 'round there and get him up, Brother," Charlotte said.

Brother left the kitchen; he was halfway across the room when Charlotte called him back. She took the bottle of beer away from him and gave him a pan of water with soap and towel.

"And be careful how you wake him up," she said. "Don't go in there with a pile of noise."

"Yes'm," Brother said.

CHAPTER FIFTEEN

Brother set the pan of water on the washstand and turned on the light. Jackson raised his head and looked at him.

"Just getting ready to wake you up," Brother said.

Jackson looked toward the door that Brother had left partially opened. He could hear the people talking and moving around in the other room. The house was so full of cracks that the voices came through the wall as clearly as if the people were on this side.

"What's going on?" he asked.

"The party," Brother said, going to the door to shut it.

Jackson sat up on the bed and passed his hands over his face. He had gone to sleep in his shorts and undershirt. The rest of his clothes were thrown over the back of a chair beside the bed.

"I was tired," he said. "How's it going?"

"All right."

He looked at Brother and smiled. He and Brother had been best of friends before he left here—they had been inseparable. He did not feel that way about Brother now, and he wondered if he ever could again.

"What time is it getting to be?"

" 'Bout eight thirty."

"How long has it been going on?"

" 'Round sundown."

"Is that water on the washstand?"

"Yeah. Miss Charlotte sunt it for you to wash your face."

Jackson passed his hands over his face again. He was still very tired. Instead of helping him, the three or four hours of sleep seemed to have made him feel worse. He felt groggy. He wished there was no party at all. What would they say when he told them he was going back? Would there be a party for him then?

He got up from the bed and went to the washstand. The warm water felt good on his face and made him feel much better. After throwing the water out through the window, he came back to the chair to get his clothes.

"Sounds like a big crowd," he said.

"Pretty good size."

He sat on the bed to put on his shoes, then went to the chifforobe mirror to comb his hair. In the mirror, he could see Brother watching him.

"Well, I guess this is it," he said, turning away from the mirror. "Listen, I might not recognize some of the people in there," he said to Brother. "How about standing close by, huh?"

Brother nodded his head. Jackson continued to look at him. He started to put his hand on Brother's shoulder, but he changed his mind. He could not make himself feel about Brother as he did before.

When they came into the other room, a woman standing by the door, threw her arms around Jackson and kissed him fully on the mouth.

"Been waiting right here just for that one thing," Olive Jarreau said. " 'Clared to the rest of 'em, I was go'n be the first one. But, my God, Jackson, you done growed up there some. Just look at you there. Just look at you. Lean here, let me kiss you again. Let me kiss you again." She kissed him on the mouth. "You see this boy trying to be bashful 'round here," she said to the rest of the people. "You see that—much bread he done ate in my kitchen.

But, my God, Charlotte got herself a man here. Ain't that little old skinny boy that left. Well, how you been, Jackson? How you been?"

"All right, Mrs. Olive."

"Yes, sir, he done growed," she said, not hearing what he had said. "And you already to start your teaching, hanh?"

He shrugged his shoulders and did not answer. Aunt Charlotte had really spread the news, hadn't she?

"I guess you have to look 'round some first," she said. "I guess that's the best. But I hope it's somewhere close so you can teach some of my great-grandchildren. You didn't know I had great-grandchildren, did you?"

"No, I didn't."

"Yes—Lord—Toni done married and got children going to school. And when you left here she wasn't nothing but a child herself. Yes, indeed. But, Jackson, you look some nice. Ain't married yet?"

"No."

"Come back to get one of your home girls, huh? Well, that's nice. Never forget the home people. No, sir, don't ever forget them. Ain't no place like home. No, sir."

"Jackson," another woman said, "your aunt busy in the kitchen, and she told me to car' you 'round to meet the people. I'm Mrs. Viney. You 'member me, don't you?"

"Yes."

"I 'member when you got baptized. You sure was a great little Christian. I hope you still keeping up the good work."

Jackson did not answer her. He could not remember the last time he went into a church. But whether or not Viney expected an answer, Jackson could not tell, because as soon as she had asked him about the church, she was introducing him to people standing close by.

Some of the people—the older ones in particular—were like Olive Jarreau; but the majority of them were not. They did not know what to do around him. He had to make the first move. If he held out his hand, they took his hand. If he spoke to them, they spoke in return. If he smiled, they did also. But when he had shaken their hands, spoken to them, smiled with them, he could not think of another thing to say or to do, and neither could they.

After Viney had introduced him to everyone in the living room, including the small children who were in school or might be starting school the next semester, and assuring them that they had better be nice because Mr. Jackson might be their teacher, she led Jackson out on the porch. The boys and girls sitting in the swing and along the railing of the porch were too interested in each other to pay Viney and Jackson any attention, and Viney led Jackson out into the yard where she hoped, as she said, the men folks would show a little more respect for someone with his learning. The men were arguing about something before they came into the yard, but as soon as Viney and Jackson came up to where they were, the conversation came to an abrupt end. The men shook Jackson's hand and spoke to him, but they did this just as the others had done. They waited for him to make the first move. He had been educated, not they. They did not know how to meet and talk to educated people. They did not know what to talk about. So let him start the conversation, and if possible they would follow. But once Jackson had spoken to them and had shaken their hands, he was as lost for words as they were. Viney noticed how uncomfortable everyone was, and she tried to start a conversation by saying that Jackson had come back here to teach. The men looked at Jackson and said, "Yes?" "Un-hun." "That's good." And that was as far as the conversation went. A long period of silence again. Everyone was waiting for someone else to do what should be done. Viney said, "Well, I guess that's all you ain't met, yet; let's go back in."

The men watched them go back up the steps, and their conversation was resumed only moments later.

CHAPTER SIXTEEN

"Well, he done met just about everybody," Viney said to Charlotte, when she came back into the kitchen. "And I reckon'd I'm go'n be heading on home."

"So soon?" Charlotte said.

"Yes. Put this old self to bed," Viney said. "If I don't see you 'fore Sunday, I'll be seeing you at church."

"Yes, I'll be there," Ch'arlotte said.

"Good night," Viney said, and went back into the living room.

"Ain't you hungry, Jackson?" Charlotte asked him.

"Not right now," he said. "Right now I'm trying to cool off."

"No wonder you hot," Charlotte said. "That coat and tie on—but I reckon'd that's what they teach y'all, though."

Jackson moved toward the screen door but did not go outside. An old woman sitting at the table raised a spoonful of gumbo to her mouth and looked at him. She drank a swallow of beer, but did not take her eyes off Jackson.

"Well, Jackson?" she said.

He looked over his shoulder for the person who had spoken to him. He recognized her immediately and came to the table where she was.

"Madame Bayonne," he said, smiling.

"Sit down," she told him.

He pulled out a chair and sat across from her. She was a tall, slim, black woman, with the sharp features of the Caucasian race. She might have been seventy years old, she might have been older. She wore a small black hat on a pile of gray hair. And she had been Jackson's teacher before he left for California.

"You are grown," she said.

"I've grown some."

"You are a man now."

"I'm twenty-two."

She looked at him closely and admiringly. He had always been her favorite student.

"You look very well yourself," he said.

"I manage to get along."

"Do you want to eat now, Jackson?" Charlotte asked him.

"Yes."

She turned away, and he heard her dishing the food; then she was back again.

"You want something to drink with it?" she asked, setting the plate before him. "Got all kinds o' soft drinks there."

"I'll take a beer," he said, looking at Madame Bayonne. But Madame Bayonne wanted no part of it, and she looked away.

"A beer?" Charlotte said.

"I drink," Jackson said, looking up at her.

"Is that nice?" Charlotte said. "And in front of the children, too?"

Jackson looked around, but saw no children watching him. He looked at Charlotte again. He could tell by her face that she was still against his drinking the beer.

"A Coke'll do," he said.

She opened a bottle of Coke for him and set the bottle and a glass on the table. She went back to the stove, and he could hear her saying something to Mary Louise about him. Both of them looked at him and Madame Bayonne sitting at the table.

"When are you going back?" Madame Bayonne asked, looking at him. Not exactly at him, he felt, but through him. She could always tell what you were feeling or thinking before you knew yourself.

How do you know I'm going back, he said with his eyes, when all the others seem to think I've come here to stay?

She did not say any more, she did not have to. She made a sound in her throat as if to assure him that he had no other choice. She raised the bottle up to her mouth, still looking through him.

"About a month," he said.

"When are you going to tell her?"

"I don't know," he said, eating. "I didn't know she expected me to come here to stay."

"You were supposed to come back," she said. She said it as though it was a vow he had broken—as though he had promised a girl he would marry her, and after she had waited ten years, he decided to back out of it.

"That was a long time ago."

"People like that never change. She remembered you said a long time ago that you would come back. She doesn't pay any attention to what is happening around her. These things mean nothing. The only important thing in her life was that you were coming back here one day."

"It's been so long since I said it."

"But you did say it. And she has been living in that dream ever since. Now you must tell her the truth."

"How?" he said.

"It's going to be hard, but you must. Do you want me to do it for you?"

"No. I'll do it myself."

"She wouldn't believe me, anyhow."

"Will she believe me?"

Madame Bayonne nodded her head. She continued looking at him—not only at him, but through him. Those eyes know everything, he thought.

"Yes, she will believe you," she said. "And it will be the worst moment of her life."

"Am I to blame for that?"

"Yes," she said.

CHAPTER SEVENTEEN

When they were through eating, they sat at the table talking a while. The people continued to come into the kitchen, but no one went to the table where Jackson and Madame Bayonne were sitting. They wanted to meet Jackson—for Charlotte's sake at least; but even for Charlotte's sake, none of them would go near Madame Bayonne. Madame Bayonne had very little to do with the people in the quarters now that she had retired from teaching, and the people, though they respected her very much, looked upon her as an eccentric old woman from whom they kept their distance. Even Brother, who got along with everybody, stood by the window with his bowl of gumbo. He had looked forward to eating at the table with Jackson, but when he saw Madame Bayonne sitting there, he had told Mary Louise that she could put his food on the shelf in the window. Mary Louise had understood, smiled, dished up the food—a bowl of rice and gumbo that could have fed three people Brother's size—and set it on the shelf before him. When the food had cooled enough so that Brother could hold the bowl in his hand, he turned away from the window with the bowl and looked at Madame Bayonne and Jackson.

"Well, I think I'll be going," Madame Bayonne said.

"Why so early?" Jackson said.

"I've seen you," Madame Bayonne said. "That's what I came for."

She leaned over to get her walking cane that lay on the floor under the table. She could not reach it, and Jackson had to get it for her.

"I'll walk with you," he said.

"No. You ought to stay. This is your party."

"I need the fresh air," he said, standing up with her. "I'll be back in a few minutes, Aunt Charlotte," he said to his aunt.

Charlotte nodded her head, but everyone in the kitchen could see that she did not like the idea of his leaving the house. She had given the party for him, to celebrate his homecoming, and he should have showed consideration by staying there. He and Madame Bayonne went through the front room toward the porch.

"You have a nice crowd," Madame Bayonne said,

when they were in the road.

"I'm sure they didn't all come to see me," Jackson said.

"They did," Madame Bayonne said, "if only to talk about it tomorrow. That's human nature."

"What's happening around here, Madame Bayonne?" he asked.

"In what way do you mean?"

"I don't know. In every way. The people, what are they doing?"

"Nothing. Now that the Cajuns have just about taken over. Nothing."

"What is this about the Cajuns taking over?"

"Just as I said. They have taken over the plantation. They have wrangled and wrangled until they have gotten everybody else to quit farming. Now those five cousins have it in their hands."

"Didn't Bud Grover—he's still alive, isn't he?"

"He's alive."

"Didn't he have anything to do with it?"

"Bud Grover is so lazy and drinks so much, I doubt if he knows where he is half of the times."

"But how did they make the people quit?"

"They kept asking for more land. Each year they showed Bud Grover where they needed more land. Bud Grover took the land from the Negroes and gave it to them."

"But why, when the Negroes were sharecropping just like the Cajuns, why?"

"White is still white, Jackson," Madame Bayonne said. "And white still sticks with white. But there are other reasons, too. This uprising by these young

Negroes now is one of them. He's proving to them
that they need him much more than he needs them.
The other reason, of course, is that the Cajuns have
always made more crop for Bud Grover than the
Negroes have. They've always had the best land—
being white they got that from the start; and they
have organization. That Villon bunch has always
worked together. Having the best land and being
able to work it all together, they grew twice as
much. When you make twice as much, you can
afford to buy more equipment, better equipment.
Once they got the equipment, they wanted more
land to work. So Bud Grover gave them the land—
acre by acre until the Negro's farm was too small to
support him. He quits, and the Cajuns get it all. The
next year another one quits; the next year another
one. Now, they've all quit. All but one."

"Raoul?"

"Yes. They're letting him run for a while—the
way you play with a fish before jerking him out of
the water."

"Why?"

"Because he's killing himself working, trying to
keep up with them. Besides he's neither white nor
black; he's not standing on a soapbox preaching
against the treatment he's getting."

"If he did?"

"He and his kind never will; you ought to know
that."

Jackson looked at the big, old house that they
were now passing. A light burned in one of the
rooms, but the rest of the house was in darkness. He

looked at the trees in the yard and he remembered how he and Catherine and Mark used to play behind the trees. He remembered how he would have to leave before Raoul came home because Raoul did not like dark people. Then, when he got home, Charlotte would whip him if she knew he had been down there, because she knew how Raoul felt, and she was afraid that Raoul would hurt him if he ever caught him there.

"I saw Catherine today," he said.

He could feel Madame Bayonne looking at him. "Did you?"

"Yes."

She was still looking at him. "You all had anything to talk about?"

"Not much."

"I'm afraid she has her hands full there," Madame Bayonne said.

"How's that?"

"You seem interested?"

"No, it's nothing," he said.

Madame Bayonne looked at him a long moment before going on. "She has two of them on her hands, three when that other one is there," she said.

"I don't understand."

"It's a long story."

"How's Mrs. Della?" he asked, after they had gone a little farther.

"She's there, but that's about all that you can say for her," Madame Bayonne said. "Catherine just about runs things now."

"Mrs. Della shouldn't be that old?"

"By years, no. But life has been hard on her. She's defeated. Finished. You remember the boy."

"Yes. He was killed just before I left."

"His memory is as fresh in that house today as it was the day it happened. Neither Raoul nor his people will ever let her forget it. I doubt if she really wants to forget him. She loved him just as much as Raoul loves Catherine. I'm sure you remember him."

"Yes."

"You fought for him enough."

"I liked his sister."

"You liked her a lot, didn't you? Or I should say you two liked each other a lot."

"I suppose so," he said, looking down at the ground—remembering.

"And now?"

"You can like a person so long," he said, but still keeping his eyes down on the ground.

"Some people like forever," she said, looking at him.

"I'm afraid I have other things to think about," he said. But Madame Bayonne thought she detected something false in the way he said it.

They were between two walls of corn now, a patch on either side of the road. It was very dark here, because the moon was behind the patch of corn on the right. Jackson could smell the sweet dry odor of the corn, and it reminded him of a field he had passed earlier that day when the bus had stopped to pick up passengers along the road, and he had opened his window for only a second.

"There was a house there once," he said, nodding to the left side of the road. "The Washingtons, didn't they live there?"

"Yes; they moved to Baton Rouge," Madame Bayonne said. "The house was torn down and everything was plowed up. That also belongs to the Cajuns.

"But it gets worse as you go farther down the quarters," she said. "Houses don't sit between houses any more; now they sit between fields. It's all right at night. It's quiet at night. But in the day you might have a tractor running up to your fence any time."

"And the people are leaving more and more?"

"Yes. Going to Baton Rouge, New Orleans. Some who have money go up North. But most of them hang around Baton Rouge and New Orleans."

"What are they doing there?"

"Whatever they can."

"There was a house there, too," he said, nodding to the field on the left again.

"Yes. Robinson. When old Robinson died, the children all moved away. I suppose they were glad he died. They hated the country, anyhow."

"Why haven't you left, Madame Bayonne?"

"Why? Moving around is for the young—the restless. I'm old now. My daughter has been trying to get me up North—Seattle. But why should I go? Let them pay me for the service I've done for this state."

"How do you make out? All right?"

"As well as can be expected. I don't have to pay rent, and I have the privilege of keeping a garden."

"Does anyone pay rent?"

"No. You can stay here for free. As long as you keep your nose clean. You don't have your farm any more—no; the Cajuns have taken that. But you can stay here if you want to."

"As long as you keep your nose clean?"

"Yes—as long as you keep your nose clean. I'm at the age now that these things don't bother me any more. I have only a few more years left, and I would love to live them in peace."

"Don't we all?"

CHAPTER EIGHTEEN

"Why did you come back, Jackson?" Madame Bayonne asked.

"Pardon me?" he said.

They were in the heart of the quarters now, and he saw what she meant about the houses and the field. Most of the houses on the left had been torn down and had been replaced by patches of corn and sugar cane. The houses that still remained looked so worn and dilapidated that Jackson knew it would be only a matter of time before they would be torn down also.

The right side of the road was different. Not only were there more houses, but they were in better condition. The yards were clean and many of them had flowers. The scent from one of the flowers—jasmine, he thought it was—permeated the air. He had heard voices from the porch as he and Madame Bayonne came up to the yard; but as they came closer, the voices ceased. Then after they had gone, the people began talking again.

"To tell her you could not come back?"

"No, it wasn't exactly that. And maybe that was part of it."

"You have finished now?"

"Yes."

"What are your plans?"

"I haven't any."

"You must have something in mind."

"Nothing concrete, Madame Bayonne."

"What will you do when you go back?"

"I don't know."

They had stopped in front of her house now—a small three-room cottage that looked no better or worse than any of the others on that side of the road. There were several little trees in the yard—flowers, too, that almost hid the house from a passerby. Madame Bayonne leaned on her walking cane and tilted her head back to look up at Jackson.

"Something is bothering you, isn't there?"

He was not looking at her; he was looking far away. He frowned and made a sound in his throat as though to say, "Do you have to even ask that?"

"There is, isn't there?" she said.

"I'm like a leaf, Madame Bayonne, that's broken away from the tree. Drifting."

"You are searching for something?"

He nodded; he was still looking away. "Yes. Searching."

She nodded now. "You were always searching. Always wanted to find something strong—something you call concrete. Always."

"Always?"

"Always," she said. "It was the same here when you were small. And even then I was afraid for you. Terribly afraid."

"Why?"

"Because you're searching for something, Jackson, that is not there. It isn't in California, and it isn't here."

"Then maybe it's some place else."

"No. It isn't there either. Men, not only black men, but all men, have looked for it, but none have found it. They have found a little of it, but not all. I'm sure some of it is in California, and some of it is here also. But all of it is not in any one place."

"I must search."

"It isn't to be found."

"I cannot bow, Madame Bayonne."

"I suppose by bowing, you mean you can't put up with the things you would have to put up with here."

He nodded. "Yes."

"Then your only alternative is to go back."

"There's no place to go back to."

"What?"

"They promised us, Madame Bayonne, they promised us. They beckoned and beckoned and beckoned. But when we went up there, we found it all a pile of lies. There was no truth in any of it. No truth at all."

"There must be some truth."

"There's no truth. They don't come dressed in white sheets with ropes. But there's no truth."

"That's why you're here?"

"I came for a while, and then to leave again. I don't know where I'm going. But it would be impossible here."

"Then it has to be there."

"Has to?"

"If you can't stay here."

He looked at her thoughtfully a moment, as though he had been thinking of some other alternative. She did not like what she saw in his face. He looked away.

"Maybe it's me."

"In a way, it is."

"In a way?" he said. "Not all the way?"

"No. Because there are many just like you. Aren't there?"

"There are."

She nodded. "I saw it in the beginning. I saw it in you then."

"I'm not looking for a paradise, Madame Bayonne."

"I know what you're looking for. Dignity, truth —you want to make something out of a senseless world."

"Is there anything wrong with that?"

She looked at him, but did not answer.

An owl suddenly left an old pecan tree about a

hundred yards from where Jackson and Madame Bayonne were standing, and went flying over the field and across the road. The owl flew so low over their heads that Jackson could almost hear the beating of its wings. He watched it fly over the house and into the night. He wondered what had caused it to leave and where it would eventually stop.

"Even he must leave sometime." Madame Bayonne had taken one quick glance at the owl, and had looked at Jackson again. "I wonder what he ever did to anyone, what was promised him, what was not fulfilled?"

Jackson turned to her. "Do you understand?"

Her eyes said it. Her mouth did not. She understood.

"Good night, Madame Bayonne," he said.

"Good night," she said.

She went into the yard, and the tall flower bushes and the trees in the yard seemed to envelope her, hiding her from him in the road. Or did these things hide the road, the outside from her? He walked away.

CHAPTER NINETEEN

The party was over. All but three people had left the house. Mary Louise and Charlotte were in the kitchen washing dishes; Jackson and Brother sat in the swing on the porch. Jackson had taken off his coat and tie and had rolled up his shirt sleeves. Brother sat beside him drinking a beer. In a rocking chair, at the other end of the porch, sat an old man sound asleep. His snoring could be heard all over the place.

It was after midnight. A heavy dew had fallen, and there was a slight breeze from the direction of the swamps. The breeze stirred the leaves in the mulberry tree at the corner of the porch.

"Finish this beer and take him in," Brother said.

"Can you handle him by yourself?"

"Oh, yeah."

"I'll give you a hand if you want me to."

"I can handle him—I do it all the time," Brother said. He raised the bottle up to his mouth, threw his head back, and drank about half of the beer. He looked at Jackson again. "Anyhow, you got something up here to take care of," he said.

"Yes, a good night's sleep," Jackson said. "And I need it."

"I mean Mary Louise," Brother said. "What you think she hanging 'round here for?"

"She's helping Aunt Charlotte with the dishes, I suppose."

"Don't take you ten years to wash no dishes," Brother said, and grinned.

He got up from the swing before Jackson could say anything, and took the empty bottle inside. When he came back on the porch, Charlotte and Mary Louise were with him.

"Done cool off," Charlotte said. "That's a blessing. Saint Ambrose still here?"

"Just getting ready to take him in," Brother said, going over to the chair where the old man sat snoring. "Okay, Saint Ambrose, let's get to getting," he said.

He pulled Saint Ambrose out of the chair, but Saint Ambrose went back down again. He pulled him back up, but again he could not keep Saint Ambrose on his feet. Jackson went over to help Brother take him out to the car.

"He must 'a' had one too many," Brother said.

"You ever knowed when he didn't?" Charlotte said.

They had a hard time getting Saint Ambrose down the steps and through the gate because he was heavy and no help to them at all. After they had gotten him into the car, Jackson shut the door. Brother went around and got in on the other side. He looked at Jackson again.

"What time you getting up tomorrow?"

"I don't know. Eight; nine."

"Probably come by and we can go riding somewhere if you want."

"Yes, that sounds all right."

Brother looked toward the porch where Charlotte and Mary Louise were, and leaned closer toward Jackson.

"Don't mean to be prying," he said; "but y'all can have that whole house to y'all self over there tonight. Herb's working in Baton Rouge."

Jackson smiled and looked away. But Brother could tell by his smile that Jackson was not interested in what he had proposed.

Brother shrugged his shoulders and sat up. "Just thought I mention it," he said, starting up the motor. "See you tomorrow."

"Take it easy," Jackson said, standing away from the car. Brother drove off, and Jackson came back into the yard.

"How did you like the supper?" Charlotte asked him.

Charlotte had dragged the rocking chair to the center of the porch, and now sat rocking and fanning with a piece of white cloth. There weren't any mosquitoes tonight, but bringing the piece of cloth along whenever she sat outside had become a ritual with her.

"All right," Jackson said.

Charlotte looked over her shoulder at Mary Louise. "Ain't you go'n sit down and cool off?"

"No'm, I ought to be going," Mary Louise said.

"I spec' you want Jackson to walk you home?" Charlotte said.

Mary Louise looked at Jackson, but did not say anything. She did not move from where she was standing either.

"Talking about shame-face," Charlotte said to Jackson. "You better take her on over there. She'll never ask you."

"About ready?" Jackson asked Mary Louise.

Mary Louise nodded and started toward the steps.

"I'll be back tomorrow when I get through at the

Yard," she said to Charlotte.

"Good night," Charlotte said, and watched them go out of the yard.

She knew she did not have anything to worry about from Mary Louise. She had watched them together tonight and she had watched them this afternoon, and she knew there was nothing between them.

CHAPTER TWENTY

When they came into the road, neither one said anything. Mary Louise wanted to talk; she had so much on her mind to talk about, but where should she begin? Where do you begin after ten years?

Actually she had not been waiting for him. She had said it many times and meant it sincerely. "No," she had said, "not him. But the first one that love me and can respect me and who I can love and respect, that's the one I'm go'n marry." But none of the boys who courted her, who took her out, seemed to be the right one.

When she took Charlotte's place at the Yard two years ago, she ceased courting altogether. All of her time was devoted to the Yard, her house, Charlotte's house, and the church. When boys attempted to escort her from church, she told them very politely that she was with someone already. If the boy insisted, Charlotte came to the rescue. Then when they were alone again, she would tell Mary Louise, "You know, you getting 'round that marrying age now. You got to spec' that kind o' 'tention."

Mary Louise would nod her head, but would not answer.

When all of her friends were getting married and asked her what was she waiting for, she told them very simply, "The right one." When they heard that Jackson was coming back—Charlotte had told everyone in the quarters that he was—and asked her if he was the one, she told them no. But he was, and he was not. One day she could not believe for a moment that he could possibly look at her. The next day she saw them together as husband and wife. One day she saw him getting off the bus with a girl walking behind him. The next day she saw him rushing toward her with opened arms. She was ready to expect almost anything.

"Thanks for what you've been doing for Aunt Charlotte," he said.

"It wasn't nothing," she said. "I was glad . . ."

She could not say any more. But why, when all the time she was bursting over with things to talk about? It was not love she wanted to talk about. No, not love at all. But him. She wanted to know about him. What had he been doing? How had he been? What were his plans now? She did not want to tell him anything about herself. Nothing interesting had happened to her. Nothing interesting had happened to the place—but that it was going down faster and faster. No; she only wanted to talk about him.

He opened the gate for her and she went into the yard. He followed her up the walk. She was going to detain him some way or another, but it was he who suggested it first.

"Can we talk a moment?"

"Yes. Want come inside?"

"No. Out here will be good."

"Let me get a chair."

"No. The steps are all right."

She used her handkerchief to wipe off a clean place for him. It was a small white handkerchief with her initials embroidered in it. A boy had given her a dozen of them for her birthday a year ago.

After sitting down, they remained silent a while. What was it he wanted to say to her? After all, he did not come back there with a wife. . . .

"How've you been?" he said.

"All right."

"You look nice."

"Been getting along all right."

"I thought you'd be married by now with a house full of kids."

"No. Still single," she said.

He leaned forward, rubbing his hands together. She looked at him, thinking: I don't care what it is. Anything—I'm ready to hear it. Say it so I can be free. Say it so I can know what to do tomorrow, so I can know how to feel tomorrow. 'Cause as long as you don't, I'll never know which way to go. . . .

"I have something to say to Aunt Charlotte," he said. "I don't know how to say it."

Mary Louise hesitated a moment before asking him what it was that he had to say.

"She thinks I'm coming back here to stay," he said.

Mary Louise's heart leaped into her throat. She stared at Jackson as if he had just confessed to murdering someone. Tears rushed into her eyes, and she raised her hand to her mouth to keep from crying out.

"How can I say it to her?" he said. "From what I hear, that's all she's been telling everyone. It's impossible. But how do I explain it?"

She had wanted to say these same words to Miss Charlotte. When he first left, everyone thought he would come back one day to teach there. Three or four years after he had gone, she still thought he would. Then suddenly all of the young people started leaving. Those who weren't being drafted or volunteering for military service were all going to the cities or up North. And she had asked herself then, why should Jackson be an exception? Why should he come back, when all of the others were going the other way? No, she had thought, he won't ever come back. I might's well get interested in somebody else 'cause I'll never see him again. So she had started dating. Different boys called on her two and three times a week. But the right one never did come along.

Charlotte might have been partially responsible for this. Not that she did not want her to get married. She definitely did want her to get married. But whenever they were together, she was continually bringing up Jackson's name and his returning. She, Mary Louise, had wanted to caution her. Several times she had wanted to say, "Miss Charlotte, you know, many o' the young people leaving and going—" but each time she thought about saying this, Charlotte would seem more confident than ever of his returning. If she showed any doubt at all, Charlotte would show her a letter from him. No, Charlotte would not let her read the letter, and whether or not Charlotte was showing her the same letter over and over, she did not know, because Charlotte would keep the letter at safe enough distance so she could not identify the date. But, nevertheless, she began to feel that maybe Charlotte was right and maybe he was an exception after all. And about two weeks ago, Charlotte did get a letter from him, for it was she, Mary Louise, who brought the letter from the store. The letter had said that he would be here next week. It did not say whether or not he was coming to stay.

"How would you do it?" he asked.

She was still crying, and did not answer him. Jackson sat up and turned to her.

"What's the matter?"

"Nothing," she said. "I don't know how to do it. Not that."

"She really thinks so?"

Mary Louise nodded her head. "Yes."

CHAPTER TWENTY-ONE

They were silent a long time. He sat forward on the steps, looking at the little beads of dew sparkling in the grass along the fence. Something pleasant stirred in him. He felt like going out there and rubbing his hand over the grass. He wanted to feel the wetness of it, he wanted to feel the soft prickling touches against the palm of his hand.

"Well, I think I ought to be going," he said.

But he did not move, and he turned to Mary Louise sitting beside him.

"Why were you crying?" he asked her.

She shrugged one shoulder. "I don't know."

"Did you expect me to come back?"

"I don't know. I reckon'd I did."

He started to tell her why he could not come back, but he was tired, and, too, could she possibly understand what he was saying? Could she understand all, not part of, but all of what he was saying about North and South? She probably would not— how could she?—when the North had been pictured for her as it had been pictured for him before he went there. But he had found out that it had its faults as well as the South. Only the faults there did not strike you as directly and as quickly, so by the time you discovered them, you were so much against the other place that it was impossible ever to return to it.

But it had taken him a long time to discover these faults, because he was too involved with his books to stand back and look for them. Hearing his mother complain about the shabby neighborhood they had to live in only because they were Negroes, or hearing his stepfather complain about his job, did not make him aware of these things either. They lived in a slum neighborhood because they did not have enough money to live in a better place, and his stepfather had to work as a laborer because he did not have the education to hold a better position. But he would not have to live under these conditions; his instructors had already told him so.

When did he begin to notice the faults? When? It was hard for him to see them when he sat in a classroom, surrounded by white students, while in the South the problem of integrating the school was causing so much trouble. It was hard to notice them when he went out for the school track team, running side by side with anyone, and then leaving most of them behind. It was hard to notice them also when he went swimming in the same pool with all the others. So when did he begin to notice them? When?

It had happened suddenly. It had sneaked up on him. No, no, it had not. It had only come less directly than it had in the South. He was not told that he could not come into the restaurant to eat. But when he did come inside, he was not served as promptly and with the same courtesy as were the others. When he went into a store to buy a pair of pants or a pair of socks, he was treated in the same manner as he had been in the restaurant. And when he and his parents were looking in the papers for another place to rent, he remembered how his mother's finger made an imprint under each place that said "colored," when all the time there were other places which she would have preferred living in and which were much cheaper. The imprint under that one word, because it was made in San Francisco, would be imprinted on his mind the rest of his life.

These incidents were not big. They were extremely small when you thought of them individually. But there were so many of them that they soon began to mount into something big, something black, something awful.

When he first went to California, it was understood by his mother and his aunt that he would go there to be educated, and then return to the South to work. But before he had finished the high school, he had become so discouraged by what he had seen and by what had happened to him that, if home were any place other than the South, he would have returned then. But there was no returning home. The North with all of her faults made it clear to you whether you were a Negro from the South, an Indian from New Mexico, or a Chinese from Hong Kong, that in spite of her shortcomings, conditions here were better than the ones you had left, or you would not have left in the beginning.

So the struggle for survival—or better yet, the struggle to keep his sanity—had begun for him. He found no help at home from parents who were continually complaining about the conditions in which they lived, and neither did he find solace in the church as he had done when he lived in the South. He was in college now, and he soon realized that he was not alone in this struggle. Not only was the red boy from New Mexico and the yellow boy from Hong Kong in it, but the white boy, born and raised in Dayton, Ohio, was in it, too.

"What is your problem?" he asked the white boy from Dayton. "You have everything."

The boy grinned and looked at him as though he were a fool.

"Look around you," the white boy said. "Look up, look down; look to your left, look to your right. Do I have anything? Do I have anything, really?"

"Then, why don't you tell them to stop? Not only what they're doing to me, but what they're doing to you, to themselves."

"Don't you think I have?" the boy from Dayton said. "Don't you think I have? I tell them with every breath I take. Your struggle is no worse than mine. I'm sure your cross is even lighter to carry."

So the struggle went on. The little incidents, the little indirect incidents, like slivers from a stick. But they continued to mount until they had formed a wall. Not a wall of slivers that could be blown down with the least wind. But a wall of bricks, of stones. A wall that had gotten so high by now that he had to stand on tiptoe to look over it.

It was then that he decided to leave before it would be impossible to look over this wall at all. He was not coming home. No, the South was not home, it had not been home for a long time now. But he had chosen the South because he knew people there, and because he had to go somewhere to think for a while. He had finished college now, and he had to leave San Francisco to think about what he was going to do from then on.

But could Mary Louise understand any of this if he tried to explain it to her? He looked at her sitting forward on the steps. He remembered how they had sat like this the night before he left for California. She was his girlfriend then, and they had exchanged many kisses, whispers, and many hugs and touches, which would have been frowned on by Charlotte if she had seen them. But sitting there beside her now, he felt none of this. He only felt a deep respect for her that he might have felt for someone in his family.

"It's getting late," he said.

"Oh, I'm not sleepy."

She looked at him and smiled. But it was hard to smile, because only a moment ago she had been crying.

"Don't you have to go to work tomorrow?"

"Yes, but couple hours' sleep all I need. Don't take me much."

"Well, I better let you get them," he said, standing up, and looking across the yard at Charlotte sitting on the porch. "Aunt Charlotte is still up."

"She'll be up till you come back."

Jackson looked at Charlotte, wondering when he would tell her he was going back. Maybe he would do so tomorrow. He did not feel like talking to anyone any more tonight. He turned to Mary Louise again.

"Well, I'll see you tomorrow," he said.

Mary Louise nodded, and Jackson went out of the yard. When he turned to shut the gate, he saw Mary Louise still sitting there watching him. He waved at her, and she waved back. Jackson walked away.

CHAPTER TWENTY-TWO

Jackson could feel the warm sun on his face. But he did not know whether it was the sun or the footsteps in the room that had awakened him. He tried to figure out what was going on without opening his eyes. The footsteps came into the room, went back out, then in, and out on the porch again. He heard someone in the road asking about him and his aunt saying that he was still asleep. He opened his eyes and he saw the opened suitcase near the chifforobe. His aunt was taking his clothes out of the suitcase and hanging them on the porch to air out.

"See you woke?" she said, coming back into the room.

"Yes."

"How did you sleep?"

"Like a log."

She went to the washstand and picked up the

deck of cards that she had found in the suitcase. She turned toward the bed with the cards.

"Gambling?" she said.

"I play a little."

"Ain't that the same thing?"

"No, we were playing whist. Some guys and I were playing on the train. Just for fun. When we separated, they gave me the cards."

"Where this go'n lead to, Jackson?"

"Everybody plays cards, Aunt Charlotte. There's no harm in that."

"Everybody don't play," she said.

"It was only for fun."

"That's how it always start. But how do it end?"

She came to the bed and sat down beside him.

"They done had mo' people killed over cards 'an anything else you can think of," she said, looking down at him. "You know that, don't you?"

"You don't have to worry about me. I'll never die over a deck of cards."

"How do you know?"

He did not answer. He reached for the deck of cards, but she drew them back and laid them on the small table beside the bed.

"I want to have a talk with you, Jackson."

"Can I get up and put on my clothes?"

"No. Stay there."

"All right," he said, and lay back down.

She did not like the way he said "all right." It was too impatient. He said it the same way he said "yes" instead of "yes, ma'am" and "no" instead of "no, ma'am." She knew he did not mean to be disrespectful when he talked like this, but she wished he would change.

"You everything, Jackson," she said. "You know that, don't you?"

A sermon coming up, he thought; and God knows I don't want to hear it.

"They ain't never been nobody in the whole family to go far's you done gone; to get your kind o' learning, to travel like you done traveled. Nobody."

She looked at him, waiting for him to say something. But he did not make the slightest gesture. He was looking across the foot of the bed toward the mantelpiece.

"In ever' family they ought to be somebody to do something. We ain't had that somebody in this family yet. All the others, they been drunks, gamblers—and your pa, there, even 'fore you was born, he had packed up and left your mon . . ."

She was silent a moment, looking at him.

"I don't mean to be preaching. You know I never liked to preach to you. I never had to, 'cause you always knowed right from wrong. But I just want you to know . . . you all they is left, Jackson. You all us can count on. If you fail, that's all for us."

Again she waited for him to say something, but he was as silent as he had been before. He had begun to perspire from the heat, and she dabbed his face with the end of the sheet.

"You still blonks to church?" she asked him.

"No."

Her heart seemed to stop beating for a moment. "How come, Jackson?"

"My subjects, I suppose."

"Your subjects?"

"My schoolwork."

"They had school up there on Sundays?"

"No. But I had to study on Sundays just like any other day."

"You couldn't take out a few minutes, Jackson?"

"I had to study. My classes were very hard. You sent me up there to study, to get a good learning. I studied."

"I didn't send you up there to quit the church."

"I had a choice. One or the other."

Charlotte looked at him and shook her head. "Don't say that, Jackson. Please don't say that."

He looked across the foot of the bed toward the mantelpiece. A calendar with the picture of Christ hung above the mantelpiece. The picture was supposed to represent Christ kneeling in the garden of Gethsemane. Jackson thought both the idea and the portrait were disgusting, and he looked away.

"Without Him, Jackson, they ain't nothing," she said. "They ain't nothing, Jackson."

"I couldn't do both," he said.

"Plenty people done done both."

"I couldn't."

She looked at him a long time, biting her lips to keep from crying.

"Jackson, I rather hear you say anything in the world 'an say that. I would."

He started not to say it, but he said it anyway. "You sent me there," he said. "I didn't want to go. I cried, I cried to keep from going. You wanted me to go. So I went. You wanted me to study, so I did."

"Yes, I wanted you to go. I wanted you to study. I wanted you to get a good learning, the kind o' learning you couldn't get here. But I didn't want you to forget God, Jackson. I didn't send you up there to do that."

"I haven't forgotten God. But Christ, the church, I don't believe in that bourgeois farce—"

Suddenly her hand came out and slapped him across the mouth. She had not intended to hit him. The hand had jerked forward to shut him up.

"I didn't hear that," she said; and tears were already running down her face. "I didn't hear that. The Lord in heaven knows I didn't hear that."

Jackson looked at his aunt and rubbed the place where she had hit him. His eyes told her if she were anyone else, he would not have taken that insult.

"I didn't hear that," she said. "Tell me I didn't hear that. Tell me I didn't hear that, Jackson." She waited. "Tell me that, Jackson."

But all he did was exhale noisily and look away. And for a long time Charlotte sat there looking down at him and crying.

"Kneel down with me, Jackson," she said. "Kneel down with me."

"I can't."

"You can't kneel?"

"I don't," he said.

"You don't even kneel?"

He was silent. Why should he say more. He had already said he didn't.

"What they did to you, Jackson? What they did to you up there?"

He was silent.

"What they did to you, Jackson?"

He was silent. He was looking toward the mantel-piece. Though he did not look for the calendar, he could see it at all times. He heard his aunt getting up off the bed and kneeling on the floor.

"Will you pray with me, Jackson?"

He did not answer her. She did not ask him again, but waited to see if he would change his mind. He remained silent, looking toward the mantelpiece. Charlotte clasped her hands together in much the same way that Christ did on the picture, and began praying. It was almost unbearable to Jackson to listen to her, but he was absolutely motionless throughout the prayer. When she was through praying, she stood up and looked at him.

"He heard me once. He sent you back. I'm sure He'll hear me again."

Jackson remained silent. Charlotte stood by the bed a moment longer and went out of the room.

Jackson stared at the calendar over the mantel-piece. Only a few days ago the calendar hung on the wall in the other room. But when Charlotte heard that Jackson was coming back, she brought it into this side. The calendar was old—her insurance man had given it to her four years ago—but it was beautiful, she thought, and there was something about looking at the Master on his knees that did something to the soul. She had thought that the picture would be encouraging to Jackson as he started out each day for his teaching.

After slipping into a pair of denim trousers and a short-sleeved shirt, Jackson stood by the window, looking into the garden. The half-dozen rows of beans that ran beside the house were nearly dry. Everything else in the garden had that half-green, half-yellow color.

I should have told her, he was thinking. I should have told her then that I'm going back. How can anyone stay here? Just look at this place. Everything is drying up; everything is half dead.

Am I any better off? Am I any more alive than either one of these hills of beans—accusing an old woman for wrecking this wretched life, and the only sin she ever committed was loving me? Am I any better off? I'm in the same class . . . dry, dead.

Part Two

CHAPTER TWENTY-THREE

URING the next few days he tried to think of a way to tell Charlotte that he was going back to California. He tried the very next day when they were sitting on the porch together; but he could not bring himself to do it. That evening when she and Mary Louise were getting ready for church, he tried then, but he could not tell her. And the next morning at breakfast—a good time to tell her, since she had already mentioned his teaching—again he failed to do so. His reason was, he told himself, he did not want to hurt her any more than he had done already. He had hurt her enough when he told her that he did not believe in the church any more.

At the same time that Jackson was trying to think of a way to tell Charlotte that he was going back to California, Charlotte was trying to get him to go to church with her and Mary Louise. But she had no more success than he did, because each time she asked him, he had something else to do, or somewhere else to go. Saturday night, he and Brother were going to a house party at Morgan Bend. Sunday night, they were going to a dance in Bayonne. Monday night, they were going to listen to a jazz band in Baton Rouge. Tuesday night,

Bayonne again. And Wednesday night, somewhere else. After the first two or three times Charlotte expected him to say no, and when he did she would look at him hopelessly and turn away. At church the people asked her about him, and she told them that any day now he would show up, but first he had to rest himself. When she and Mary Louise were walking back home, she would say, "I hate lying to these people like that, but what else can I say?"

"He might come yet," Mary Louise would say.

"I doubt it," Charlotte would say.

But the following day she would ask him again, and again he would have somewhere else to go.

In the afternoon when it was cool, he went for walks across the field. But he hardly recognized the old place any more. The old houses that had once stood back there had been torn down. Many of the trees had been cut down and sold for lumber and firewood, and the places where he used to pick pecans and blackberries were now plowed under. Patches of corn, cotton, and sugar cane had taken the place of everything. He would stand on one of the headlands, trying to remember whether or not a house once stood in a certain place, but there was nothing there to assure him that it did, and later that afternoon, just before sundown, he would start back for the quarters. If he thought Charlotte had already left for church, he would go directly home. If not, he would stop at Madame Bayonne's. Madame Bayonne was always glad to see him, and as soon as he came in, she offered him something to eat or a glass of her homemade wine. Jackson would accept the wine, and he and Madame Bayonne would sit at the kitchen table drinking and talking. Madame Bayonne wanted to hear his opinion of the Freedom Riders and the sit-in demonstrations by the Negro students in the South. He would sit there talking with her until he was sure that Charlotte had left, then he would leave for home. He would find his food dished and sitting on the back of the stove where Charlotte had left it to keep warm. After eating he would go to his room to read or out on the porch to sit in the swing. If Brother showed up later, they would go out riding somewhere and would not return until after midnight. Usually Charlotte would be waiting up for him on the porch. If Mary Louise was out there with her, Jackson would sit with them until Mary Louise got ready to leave. If Charlotte was out there alone, Jackson would speak to her, linger a moment, and go into his room. Since he could not make up his mind to tell her he was going back, he kept away from her as much as he could.

CHAPTER TWENTY-FOUR

Mary Louise seemed to stay at the house now. Before going to work each day she stopped by the house to see if Jackson was up. When she came from work in the afternoon, she stopped by the house before going home. If Jackson was not there, she would talk to Charlotte until he came back. If he did not show up before it was time for her to go to church, then after church she would come back to the house again. She was constantly reminding herself that it was only a friendship affair. That was what he wanted, and she would not make anything else of it. After all, where could it go? He was leaving within a few weeks, and what would become of it then? No, he was right. It should not be any more than what it was.

But something happened to her whenever they were alone. If Charlotte or Brother was there, everything seemed to go all right. But whenever he and she were alone, she felt tense and nervous. Once he brushed against her, and she drew away from him as if she had touched something hot. He had not noticed this at all; he had never stopped talking.

They usually talked about the place and about old people who had died and about those who had moved away. If she asked him anything about the other place, he would shrug his shoulders as if the other place did not exist.

Sometimes they went to the store together. She felt good walking beside him. No, he was not her man, but she could pretend he was, since no one else knew he was going back.

She never talked about his going back. She never talked about the church with him. Many times she thought she should, since he and Miss Charlotte did not seem to be able to talk to each other, but then she did not want to irritate him. She knew he had left the church, and to mention it to him might have made him angry. She would do nothing to spoil their friendship.

One day while they were at the store drinking a Coke, Catherine Carmier came out there. Catherine and Jackson looked at each other in a way that she did not particularly like; then Catherine went inside the store. When she came back out, she walked past them as though they were not even there.

"Y'all ain't speaking?" Mary Louise asked.

Jackson only smiled. When they were through drinking their Cokes, Jackson took the empty bottles inside, and he and Mary Louise started down the quarters.

I see, Mary Louise thought. They in love. That's it. They in love.

"Church again tonight?" he asked her.

"Yes. Every night for another month or two."

"How many candidates do you have?"

"Two."

"When is baptism?"

"September."

"I'm sure you'll have many more by then," he said. "Especially with you praying for them."

She looked up at him, and something seemed to grip her heart. But why should she feel that way? Why? He was going back, wasn't he? And wasn't it she who was walking in the street with him, and not Catherine? So why should she feel cheated?

When they came up to the house, they saw Charlotte sitting out on the porch. Mary Louise sat down in the swing, but Jackson went inside the house.

"How was the walk?" Charlotte asked.

"Fine. Went to the store."

"I saw y'all coming from there time you turned down the quarters. Look like y'all had a lot to talk about."

"Just talking," Mary Louise said.

Charlotte continued looking at her. Mary Louise felt uncomfortable, and pressed her foot against the floor to move the swing.

"What do y'all talk about, Mary Louise?"

Mary Louise shrugged her shoulders. "Things, that's all."

"What kind o' things?"

"Nothing much, Miss Charlotte."

"About y'all?"

"Jackson don't have no interest in me."

"Then what?" Charlotte demanded.

Mary Louise looked at the old woman, and for the first time in her life she felt afraid of her. She had been around Charlotte ever since she could remember, and Charlotte had never spoken to her so roughly before.

"I guess it ain' no business o' mine," she said. "Just like nothing else 'round here don't seem to be no business o' mine."

She turned away, and Mary Louise saw her raise her hand up to her face. Mary Louise wanted to ask if anything was the matter, but remained silent. Charlotte passed her hand over her forehead and over her temples. When she brought her hand down to her lap, Mary Louise noticed her frowning as though she had a headache.

"Miss Charlotte?"

"I'm all right," Charlotte said, and looked down the quarters. "Well, I better get ready for church." She turned to Mary Louise again. "You going?" she asked.

"Yes'm," Mary Louise said.

Charlotte got up to go inside. Mary Louise sat in the swing a few minutes longer, thinking that Jackson might come back out there. When he did not, she left the house.

She stopped just before going into her yard. Someone stood on Raoul Carmier's front porch looking at her. At first she thought it was only a white dress hanging on the line, but after moving closer to the gate, she saw that it was Catherine.

I feel sorry for you, you fool, Mary Louise thought. He going back, and even if he wasn't, it'd be just like the other one you had. He ain't go'n never let you have nobody.

She went into the yard, leaving Catherine standing on the porch watching her. A few minutes later she returned with a flashlight. Charlotte met her at the gate, and they went down the quarters together.

CHAPTER TWENTY-FIVE

Jackson and Madame Bayonne were sitting on the porch when Catherine and Lillian went past the house with the boy walking between them. Catherine spoke to Madame Bayonne and Madame Bayonne waved back at her. Both she and Jackson watched them go down the quarters.

It was a nice afternoon with flakes of cloud hiding the sun. A little wind had tried to stir a couple of times, but each time it lasted only a moment, then passed away again. Jackson sat on the floor with his back against a post, watching Madame Bayonne shell a pan of dry beans. Two sacks were on the floor next to her chair—one with unshelled beans, the other with beans that had already been shelled. Jackson liked watching the smooth, easy movements of Madame Bayonne's fingers as they split open and ran through each pod.

"Why didn't she speak to you?" Madame Bayonne asked. "I'm sure she saw you there."

"I don't know."

"Don't you?" she asked, looking down at him.

"I don't."

"What happened, Jackson?"

"No idea."

"She spoke to you the first day you came—you all talked the first day you came. You said so yourself."

"We did."

"Then why not today?"

"Maybe she didn't see me," he said, smiling.

"Sure," Madame Bayonne said.

She looked at him long enough to shred two pods of beans and drop the empty shells on the floor; then she looked in the direction that Catherine had gone.

"She doesn't usually walk down the quarters like this—especially with that child," Madame Bayonne said. She turned to Jackson again. "I wonder who she's interested in showing that child to."

"Search me," Jackson said, shrugging his shoulders and looking at Madame Bayonne. Each was playing cat and mouse with the other and both knew it. "Whose child is it?" he asked. Already he was afraid what the answer might be.

"Hers," Madame Bayonne said, looking down at him and wondering what it was between him and Catherine. No, not what it was; she knew what it was. It had always been there. Catherine had a red coat then and a long braid of black hair that hung down her back like a twisted rope. And he had a leather coat then and one of those little caps with the flaps on either side to cover his ears when it was cold. So she knew what it was all the time. Now she wondered when and how they had gotten the chance to be alone.

Jackson glanced in the direction that Catherine had gone, but he could not see her for the flowers and trees in the yard. He looked at Madame Bayonne again—casually; he did not want her to see what was in his face. But she knew what would be there even before he looked at her.

"She's not married," she said. "No; he ran the boy away before he had a chance to marry her."

She watched his face, waiting to see what, if any, change it would take. He became angry, tried to check himself, but was unable to do so. I see, she thought. I see. So that's it, huh?

He lowered his head and Madame Bayonne looked away.

"From the day he found out that Della's second child was not his, Catherine has been the only person in the world to mean anything to him," Madame Bayonne said. "Della is no more than a servant around that house, and that other one doesn't mean anything to him at all. I suppose it was wrong from the beginning. Della had no more business marrying Raoul than I would have marrying him. She's nothing like Raoul, and she's nothing like his people. Their color? Yes, their color. But color is only skin deep, and below that Della is as much Negro as you or I. Raoul is not. No, he's not white either. He hates one as much as he does the other. But his idea—his idea of what things are about as opposed to her idea—is what I mean. Do you see?"

He was looking at her now. He did not answer, but he thought he understood what she was getting at.

"They are an antithesis—at opposite poles. No, not color. Wipe color out of your mind. Color will be forgotten—eventually. The idea, the idea . . ."

He nodded—not really a nod, but a motion almost infinitesimal, to assure her he understood.

"Della was happy when she first came up to that house. She was happy in the way that only a few people can be happy. There was no fear of anything; she had a decent word to say to anyone who went by that house. Not only a few people, but many, many have stood in front of that gate talking to her. She could lean on that gate talking for hours on end.

"Then it all stopped. It stopped without warning. One day she was talking to you, the other day she was not. Everyone knew what had caused the change—Raoul; and everyone accepted it. Only she could not. For a while—yes; then it started again. Only this time it was with one person, and this time it was at night."

She looked at him.

"I know what you're thinking. She was wrong. Yes, she was wrong. But it was not then that she was wrong. She was wrong when she came to that house. It was wrong when she said 'I do,' when all the time she should have been saying 'I don't.'

"So she went to him—the other one. And if God knows what she saw in that nigger, I don't know. I'm sure if she had picked up a chunk of wood and thrown it over her shoulder at random, anything she would have hit would have been a hundred times better than Bayou Water. If he wasn't the most trifling thing that God ever put on earth, he was next to it. And he proved it as soon as he found out she was pregnant. I doubt if she was through getting the words out of her mouth before he was packing the handbag and getting away from here.

"Della did not want Bayou Water. She did not love Bayou Water. But she needed Bayou Water. Not necessarily Bayou Water, but someone. Though Raoul had made her stop leaning on that gate, he did not think one moment about staying there and being with her himself."

Madame Bayonne was silent a moment before continuing.

"Raoul has been Della's husband only by law. Other than that, it's been the land. Not Della he loved when he married her—the land. Della was brought there to cook his food, to bear his children, to see that his clothes were kept half clean. . . . Why the land, you ask? Why the land? It happened long before Raoul was born. Probably his great-grandfather was the first one to find out that though he was as white as any white man, he still had a drop of Negro blood in him, and because of that single drop of blood, it would be impossible to ever compete side by side with the white man. So he went to the land—away from the white man, away from the black man as well. The white man refused to let him compete with him, and he in turn refused to lower himself to the black man's level. So it was to the land where he would not have to compete—at least side by side—with either. He was taught to get everything from the land, which he did, and which he, through necessity, was taught to love and to depend upon. His love for his land, his hatred for the white man, the contempt with which he looks upon the black man has passed from one generation to the other. Robert brought it here, and you see it in Raoul.

"Raoul did not choose his position. He did not choose that house up there behind those oak and pecan trees. He is only carrying out something that was cut out for him in the beginning. He has no control over it. He was not put there by Robert, nor his grandfather. He was put there by the white and the black man alike. The white man will not let Raoul compete with him because of that drop of Negro blood, and at the same time he has put the Negro in such a position that Raoul would rather die than compete with him. So it is Raoul alone— Raoul and his land, his field. Pass me that sack, will you?"

He held the sack open for her. She poured the shelled beans into the sack. Then he refilled the pan with beans from the other sack, and moved back against the post again.

"No; Della was for convenience sake. To look after the house, to bear his children, and other than that—nothing. But that was not enough for Della. She could not shut herself away from the world. She had that single drop of blood in her just as he had, but she was taught from the beginning the direction that she would have to take. By the time she came here, she had accepted that direction— fate, if you'd rather call it fate.

"The first child, as you know, was Catherine— his. But he and everyone else knew that the second one was not. And from the moment he found this out, Catherine has been the only person in the world. to mean anything to him. There's no one else. There can't ever be anyone else."

CHAPTER TWENTY-SIX

"His people took that other gal away from there when she was small, and when they were sure she was his. But he would not let Catherine out of his sight. She went to school in that church up there until she finished the eighth grade, and that was all the schooling she got. Every now and then he would let her go to New Orleans, Baton Rouge, or visit some of her people in Bayonne; but other than that—nothing. And no one comes there to visit him. No relatives—and a boy is plumb out of the question. He feels that the boy might get her to leave, and when and if this happens, that will be the end of him.

"If that boy had been his, it would have made all the difference in the world. With people like Raoul, more so than with others, a son is the most important thing in his life. He's a loner from the beginning—but that son would be there to stand beside him. That son would be there to lessen this load of loneliness. He would be there to continue whatever he had started and was unable to finish. But this was not his son—this boy was black. And instead of lessening this load, the presence of the boy increased the burden.

"So he went to Catherine. She was to be victim now, cross-carrier now, as long as he was alive. If she goes for a visit, she must hurry back or he goes after her. When he's sick, it must be her hand which puts the medicine in his mouth. You know this already, because he was sick once when you were here. He stayed on his back a whole month, and he kept her from school every day until he was up again. Sure, Della could have brought him the cough syrup or made the tea or broth—whatever was necessary. But, no, the boy was black. If he were white, it would have been the same. They have put her in this position—behind those trees—and nothing, hear me clearly, Jackson, nothing outside those trees is allowed in that yard." She stopped, looked at him a moment, and went on. "Not too long ago—three years, I'd say—he hired a bunch of Creoles to help him get in his crop. Catherine fell in love with one of them and became pregnant. When the boy found out he came there for her. If that boy ever made a bigger mistake in his life, I'm sure he hasn't made two. The only thing that kept Raoul from killing him was Della and Catherine getting in the way long enough for him to get out of that yard. He went back to Baton Rouge and wrote for Catherine to follow him. He wrote and wrote and wrote, but she would not go."

Madame Bayonne stopped, and looked at Jackson a long moment. "Do you know why?"

He did not answer her. He was unable to answer her. She continued to look at him.

"She cannot leave that house, Jackson. Do you understand what I'm trying to say to you? She cannot leave that house."

It did not make any sense to him at all. Neither

what she was saying, nor the way he was feeling. He did not care about antithesis at the house, but he did care about his feeling. He did not like the way he was feeling. He was feeling in a way that he had told himself he had no right to feel. To fall in love—not to fall in love—but to be in love with Catherine was impossible. He had other things to do. Love was for those who were ready to settle down, to accept what was handed out. He was not. And yet he had been feeling this way ever since he saw her. Something like an electric current had hit him the moment he laid eyes on Catherine. It was impossible to hide it, and at the same time he knew to feel this was insane.

"And you're sure nothing happened?" Madame Bayonne asked, looking down at him.

"Nothing."

"Think," she said, continuing to look down at him. She knew all the time that something had happened. "Think hard. Maybe you all brushed against each other at the store. Maybe you touched her arm—accidentally. Maybe she just slightly stepped on your foot. Are you sure none of these things happened? It doesn't take much, you know, to arouse an old flame. Did she see you and that other gal holding hands somewhere?"

He knew she was making fun of him now, and he neither looked at her, nor would he answer her.

"Pass me that sack," she said.

He held the sack open for her and refilled the pan, but he did not raise his head. Farther up the quarters the first bell rang for church.

"A day, a day," Madame Bayonne said. "They come and go faster now."

"And I think I'll be going," Jackson said.

Madame Bayonne looked at him. "Leaving?" she said.

"Yes, I think so."

CHAPTER TWENTY-SEVEN

When he came into the road, he saw Catherine, Lillian, and the child coming back up the quarters. He would have turned away without speaking, but they had already seen him.

He did not want to walk up the quarters with Catherine. He would not have minded going up there with Lillian—Lillian did not matter—but not with Catherine. But now what could he do? Turn his back and walk away? And what would they think of him? Maybe they would figure out his motive; maybe they would think he was afraid of what the people would say if they saw them together.

He watched them come closer. Catherine held onto one of the child's hands; Lillian held onto the other. Nelson walked with his head down, dragging his foot in the dust. Just before they came up to the gate where he was, he heard Madame Bayonne calling his name. He went back into the yard.

Madame Bayonne looked down at him from her chair. Her hands continued to shred the beans, but her eyes were fixed on him. The eyes were telling him something, but he pretended not to understand.

"You have to go up there now?"

"They're waiting for me."

The eyes—those eyes which could look through you—were still fixed on him. They could say much more than the mouth ever could. He still pretended not to understand.

"A word to the wise—" she started, then stopped. "Don't go behind those trees, Jackson. It won't come to any good."

But now he would go. Nothing would keep him from going now.

"You must prove you're not afraid of him, huh?" Madame Bayonne said. "What about her? What about your aunt?"

He remained silent—standing there as though he was waiting to be dismissed. She understood.

"They're waiting," she said, jerking her head toward the gate.

He turned away. When he came into the road, he found them standing in front of the gate. He saw Catherine waving at Madame Bayonne; by the look in her face, he could tell that Madame Bayonne waved back at her. They started walking. He walked beside Lillian. He was closer to Lillian when he came out of the yard, but even if he had not been, he probably would have moved over to where she was.

"How did it go?" he said to Lillian.

"All right."

"How've you been? Haven't seen you since the first day you came."

"Can't complain," Lillian said. "And yourself?"

"About the same."

This was all they could think of to say. For the next few minutes, there was nothing but silence. Though Catherine and Lillian did not seem to mind the silence, he hated it very much. It made him feel foolish and uncomfortable.

To make matters worse, he saw that the people were watching them as they went farther up the quarters. From doors, from windows, from their porches, the people stared at them. Some of those who had been sitting in chairs and on the floor stood up to watch them go by.

"What have you been reading?" he asked Lillian. He did not care about Lillian's reading, he wanted to break the silence.

Lillian started with Victor Hugo, whom she was reading at present, then she went to Dumas, whom she had read only recently. Dumas, like Pushkin, her favorite poet, was part Negro. Did Jackson know about that?

Yes, he did.

He had said yes as though he was waking out of a sleep. Maybe he was, because he had not heard half of what Lillian had said. All the time that Lillian was talking, he was thinking about Catherine on the other side of her. He was walking near the ditch with his head down, but each time he looked up, he had to look over to where she was. Once when he did so, she happened to be looking at him at the same time. His heart seemed to jump in his throat, and he turned his head away quickly.

Lillian had caught Jackson and Catherine looking at each other, and she had felt good about it. Maybe this was what it would take to get her away from that house. Maybe this was it.

It was Lillian and not Catherine who had suggested that they go for a walk in the quarters. They had both seen Jackson go by the house, and Lillian could tell from Catherine's face that she wanted to be near him. Only Catherine did not know what excuse to use to get out of the yard. Lillian had suggested a walk. At first Catherine had seemed skeptical, but she had later agreed. Poor Catherine did not know what was ticking away in Lillian's mind. If she did, she probably would have hated her for it.

When they came up to the gate—they had gotten there sooner than anyone realized—Lillian told Jackson that she wished she would see him again, then she took Nelson by the hand and led him away. She had done all of this so suddenly that Jackson did not have a chance to say anything to her. He and Catherine were alone.

"Well, I guess I'll be going," he said. He said it in a voice that sounded too nervous and too hoarse to be his own.

"Why don't you come by sometime?"

He looked at her. He could not believe that she really meant what she had said. She did not repeat it. Maybe it had slipped out of her mouth because this was the normal thing that one person would say to another.

"How long are you going to be here?" she asked him.

"A couple more weeks."

"Maybe I'll see you again," she said. But from the look in her face, this was not half of what she had wanted to say. No, not nearly half. Maybe this was not it at all. Maybe she wanted to say something else—and maybe nothing. Maybe what she really wanted was to feel his arms around her, their bodies pressed together, his mouth on her mouth. No, not maybe, this is what both of them wanted.

They continued to look at each other. Then a little smile came on her mouth. It seemed to say—All right, nothing can come of our love, but we can like each other, can't we? They can keep us apart, but they can't make us stop liking each other, can they? Then the smile went away, and her eyes said: Liking is not enough for us, is it? Is it? No, his eyes said. No. But we must understand, mustn't we? her eyes said. His eyes did not answer. Mustn't we? her eyes said. But he still did not answer. Only his heart seemed to tell him that she was right.

"Good night," she said.

It was a while before he knew that she had spoken, and even when he did, it was a while, yet, before he could draw himself away from her.

"Catherine," he said, nodding.

She went into the yard, and he walked away, and there was an emptiness in him deeper than he had ever known before.

CHAPTER TWENTY-EIGHT

Charlotte had already left for church when Jackson got home. He went into the kitchen and ate, but he ate only a little. When he was through eating and had washed his plate, he came out on the porch again. He sat in the swing and looked at the big house farther down the quarters. Dusk was just setting in, but the trees around the old house made the place look as black as pitch. The emptiness was still in him, and he tried to make it go away by telling himself that all of this was nonsense. He told himself that he could not think of this now. He told himself that there were more important things to think about. He had to think about his future. He had come here for that purpose—not to fall in love. But the emptiness would not leave him, because regardless of whatever else he tried to think about, he could not get her out of his mind.

He sat on the porch a long time, looking at the house farther down the quarters. He wanted to go back down there again; he wanted to see her again; he wanted to see that love for him in her eyes; he wanted to see that little smile again. But he knew he should not even think about it.

When he saw Charlotte and Mary Louise coming home from church, he went inside and lay across the bed. But the emptiness was with him when he got up the next morning, and it was with him all day. He went for a walk along the river, and it was with him there also. I know better, he told himself. I know better. Don't you see how it is? Don't you see? I want something, don't you see? I want to be something, don't you see? And all you would do is get in my way—block me. Don't you see that once I'm tied down, it is all over? That I must take what they give to me whether I want to or not?

He picked up pebbles and threw them into the water. He watched the circles get bigger, bigger until they had disappeared. He found that tossing pebbles and watching the circles disappear helped him in his thinking. Yet, it did not solve anything.

That evening he sat on the porch, looking at the house. The sun was just going down, giving everything an orange and purplish color. He felt lonelier than ever before. It is like this with people who are in love. The setting of the sun is the worst time of day.

He could not sit there any longer. He would have to go for a walk. If he did not see her, then he would see the house. He would see the gate; he would see the place where they stood the day before.

His heart pounded in him as he came up even with the house. She was sitting on the porch. She was there alone. Did she look at him, or was it his imagination? He came back. Yes, she had stood up and she was looking toward the road. He came back again. She was at the gate. His heart raced so fast when he saw her that he thought he would be unable to stay on his feet. But he managed to say, "Care to go for a walk, Catherine?"

She came into the road where he was and they went back up the quarters. He did not know where they would go, but as they came up to his house, he opened the gate and they went into the yard.

"The first time you've been here?"

"Yes," she said.

"How's it been? All right?"

"All right," she said.

They were sitting on the steps. They were silent after this. Catherine sat forward with her hands clasped together, and Jackson could tell that she was not comfortable being at the house. But he did not know what to say or to do to make her feel at ease.

"It's wrong, I suppose?"

"Yes," she said. She was not looking at him; she was looking down at the gate.

"I know," he said. He waited for her to disagree with him, but she did not. "I told myself that. I kept telling myself that. But it didn't do any good."

She looked at him and looked toward the gate again.

"Were you expecting me to come by?" he asked.

"I was hoping."

"Were you really?"

She did not say any more. Maybe she should not have said that much.

He continued to look at her. His heart was beating fast in him. He had never felt this way about anyone before. He wondered if he should move closer to her. He wanted to. He wanted to touch her arm; he wanted to touch her face.

A man went by the house, and Jackson saw Catherine draw back a little. The man had not seen her; he had not even looked in that direction.

"I ought to be going," she said.

"He didn't see you."

"I ought to be going anyhow."

She stood up to leave, and he stood up with her. Just before going through the gate, he pulled her back and kissed her. She did not respond to him. He thought he had frightened her because of his awkwardness, and he kissed her again. It was the same as before.

"What is the matter, Catherine? What is the matter? You came to me."

She looked at him—wanting him. Yet she was afraid to give back.

He kissed her again.

"Is it him?" he asked.

"Let's go."

"Is it?"

She was silent.

"Will I see you again?"

"I don't know."

"I must know."

"You know it's wrong, don't you? Don't you know it's wrong? All we can do is hurt each other, don't you know that?"

"Say you don't love me, Catherine, and I'll never see you again. Say you don't love me, and I'll never bother you again."

She looked at him—silence.

"Say it, Catherine. Say it."

"You know how I feel."

"Yes," he said, nodding. "Yes."

He passed his hand over her hair and her face. Her mouth brushed against his hand. Was it an accident, or was she actually kissing him? They went out of the yard.

"Will I see you again?"

"I don't know."

They were walking fast to keep from meeting anyone in the road. When they came up to the other house, they stood in front of the gate.

"Can't you leave the house tomorrow night? Can't you go in the car somewhere?"

"I shouldn't. You know that."

"Yesterday you even invited me to the house. Why?"

"I don't know."

"You do know."

She looked away.

"All right," he said. "I won't insist. I don't even want to love you. You can only get in my way. You know that? Only in my way. But I can't help myself. I do love you. I need you. And you need me, Catherine."

She would not look at him.

"All right," he said. "I'll leave."

He turned to go.

"Jackson?" she said.

He turned to her.

"I'll be there."

CHAPTER TWENTY-NINE

Della was sitting on the porch when Catherine came into the yard. Nelson was sitting in his little rocking chair next to her. Catherine would have gone by without saying anything to either one of them, but Della stopped her.

"Do you know what you're doing?"

"I only went for a walk."

"Yes, and up there," Della said, looking at her. "I warned you yesterday, I'm warning you again—"

"I'm not married to Daddy, Mama."

"Oh," Della said. "You not?"

Catherine started inside.

"I didn't say I was through," Della said.

Catherine did not answer her. She went into her room and lay across the bed. A moment later, Lillian came into the room where she was.

"Went somewhere?" Lillian asked. "I came out on the porch looking for you, but you weren't there."

Catherine lay on the bed facing the wall, and she did not answer Lillian. Lillian had gone out on the porch, as she said, but she knew all the time that Catherine and Jackson had gone back up the quarters. She had stood at the window watching them.

"Was it Jackson?" she said. "Did you all go somewhere?"

Catherine was silent. Lillian lay on the bed beside her.

"What's the matter, Cathy? If you love him, why not?"

Catherine did not say anything, and Lillian put her arm around Catherine's shoulder.

"I'm with my sister," she said. "I'm with my sister whatever she does."

"Go to your room, Lillian," Catherine said.

"Don't send me away, Cathy," Lillian said.

"Go to your room," Catherine said.

"Please, Cathy."

Catherine did not say any more. She was still facing the wall. Lillian lay beside her a moment longer, then she stood up. She looked down at Catherine, leaned over and kissed her, and went out of the room.

Catherine got up from the bed and sat down in front of the dresser. She turned on the little white lamp to her left, and looked at herself in the mirror. I feel like a bitch, she thought. Every time I look at a man, I feel like a bitch. She picked up the long-handled brush and began brushing her hair. Her hair was long and nearly black, and she loved brushing it. After she had passed the brush through her hair the number of times she usually did every night, she gave it six extra strokes for safekeeping and laid the brush to the side. She picked up her small hand mirror, held it up and out, then turned a little to look at the right side of her face. Then she turned the other way to look at the left side. She lifted her hair in back, held it over her head, then to the side. She laid the small mirror on the dresser and turned to the larger one in front of her. She was not through with her hair yet. She pulled it to the side, twisted it, and pinned it on top. Then she unpinned it, twisted it, rolled it, and pinned it in back. She unpinned it again and tied a ribbon around it so that it would hang in a pony tail. She stopped and looked at herself; then she jerked the ribbon out of her hair and threw it on the floor.

She was lying across the bed when she heard the car come into the yard. Nelson was asleep beside her. She looked at him and went back to the kitchen. The clock on the shelf had ten thirty. Catherine turned on the stove and set a pot of water over one of the burners to boil.

"Still up?" Raoul said when he came in.

"Wasn't sleepy," she said.

Raoul set a big cardboard box of groceries on the table and began taking the things out and putting them on the shelf against the wall.

"Like some tea?" Catherine asked him.

"Sounds all right."

Catherine dropped enough bay leaves in the water for two cups of tea. She stood over the stove, watching the water turn from clear to light brown. When she thought the leaves had boiled enough, she poured two cupfuls and brought them to the table.

"Cakes there," Raoul said.

She got the bag of vanilla wafers off the shelf and put some on a plate. She brought the plate to the table and sat across from Raoul.

"Saw any of the people?" she asked.

"Saw Margaret. Didn't go by Elvira."

"Saw Jeanette?"

"She wasn't there."

Catherine drank some tea and looked across the table at Raoul.

"What's the matter?" he asked her.

"Huh?" she said absently. "Nothing."

Raoul continued to look at her. The two of them had been around each other so much that each could tell when the other was holding back something. Raoul did not say any more.

When he was half through with his cup of tea, Raoul looked out of the door. Catherine raised her eyes and looked at him. She could look at him more closely now. When he was facing her, it was impossible to do so. He could read her mind too well.

Raoul began talking about the field. Whenever he talked about the field now, the Cajuns and their tractors always got into the conversation. He was afraid, and Catherine could tell. He was the only colored farmer holding out against them now, and he knew that sooner or later they were going to take over. But he was not ready to let them take over yet. If he had to work seven days a week, twelve hours a day, he would do it. He was going to give them hell before their tractors plowed dirt in his face.

Catherine looked at him. She was proud of him when he talked this way, and yet, she was afraid. She knew what the Cajuns could do when someone got in their way. They had proved this when her grandfather stood up against them. She knew they would not hesitate to do the same thing to Raoul.

But she had waited up tonight for a special reason. Tonight she wanted to look at Raoul closely. She wanted to decide whether her entire life should be devoted to him, or whether she should be free to look at someone else. She knew she could not leave them—that was impossible as long as he and Della remained the way they were toward each other; but she wanted to know if she should see Jackson again. If she did see him, she wanted to do so without feeling ashamed; she wanted to see him and not feel like a bitch afterward.

Raoul leaned back in his chair and looked out into the yard. He drank from his cup of tea and narrowed his eyes into two small slits. He seemed thoughtful one moment, then worried the next. How can I decide anything when he's like this? Catherine asked. How? Raoul sat up in the chair and looked at her again.

"Well, I better turn in," he said.

"Turning in?"

Raoul drank the last of the tea.

"You sure you got nothing on your mind?" he asked her.

"Nothing," she said.

"Well, I'm turning in."

After he had gone, Catherine washed the two cups, put them away, and went to her room. She took off her clothes and lay beside the baby. Nelson was asleep, snoring soft and evenly. Catherine lay on her side, looking at him. She passed her hand over his hair and the side of his face. She caressed his ear with her finger, kissed it, and turned on her back.

Catherine thought about Raoul and Jackson. What could she do? It was impossible to belong to both at the same time, and it was just as impossible to belong to one and not to the other.

CHAPTER THIRTY

Catherine sat near the end of the porch; Della was next to her, near the door; and Raoul sat across from both of them. They had been sitting on the porch half an hour and there had not been a dozen words spoken between them. Every now and then Della would slap at a mosquito with the piece of cloth that she had brought out of the house, but other than this, there was nothing from any one.

It had become extremely dark by now, but Catherine could see someone coming up the road. When he passed the first gate, he stopped a moment, then walked on. Catherine knew who it was, and a few minutes later, he returned, stopped, and went back up the quarters.

"I think I'll go for a ride in the car," she said to no one in particular, but loud enough for both Della and Raoul to hear. "I wonder if Lily would like to go."

She had to pass by Della to go inside the house. Della looked up at her as she came up to the door, and she could tell that Della had seen Jackson too.

Lillian was lying across the bed reading a magazine when Catherine came into the room. Lillian made an imprint on the page with her fingernail and turned on her side to look at Catherine. She was smiling already—it was a habit with her. She felt that Catherine had more troubles than her share, and it was her, Lillian's, duty to give Catherine her undivided attention whenever Catherine approached her. There was nothing hypocritical about this. Lillian was sincere toward Catherine in every way.

"Want to go for a ride?" Catherine asked her. "I'm going up the road a piece."

"Is it Jackson?" Lillian asked.

Catherine did not answer. At that moment, she hated both Lillian and herself. Herself, for feeling like a bitch; Lillian, for loving what she was doing.

"No, I don't think so," Lillian said, knowing that it was Jackson, and knowing that Catherine was asking her only as an excuse.

"Lily, can't you go out there one night? Can't you sit out there with them one night?"

Lillian looked from Catherine down to the bed. Catherine knew it was no use discussing it, and she went out of the room. She stood in the hall, trying to decide, now, whether or not to go. She wanted to go, she needed to go, but she felt, too, that she ought to be here. She ought to be on the porch with them, sitting between them, talking to both of them, and making them talk to each other. She knew that five minutes after she was gone, one would find an excuse to leave the porch. No, not one; he would. It was always he who left, as though he must, not from hatred as much as a feeling of guilt, get away from her. Was it the boy? Was it Mark? And was that who Della was thinking about all those hours that she was silent? No, she should not go anywhere. She should never even think about going anywhere— but a moment later she was driving out of the yard.

She saw Jackson standing at the gate in front of the house. He must have seen the car come out of the yard. She drove by him slowly, without stopping, because she knew they could see the lights from the house. He must have understood why she did not stop, and he ran to the other side of the car, opened the door as she slowed up, and jumped in.

"One way of killing myself," he said.

She looked at him, smiled, but did not say anything. When she came out on the highway, she turned the car toward Bayonne.

"Do you want me to drive?" he asked her.

She drove to the side and stopped. He got out, went around to the other side and got under the steering wheel.

"Would you like a beer?" he asked. "I know a place a few miles from here?"

"I wouldn't mind having one," she said.

He drove up the highway two or three miles, then turned off on a black tar road. The road was walled in by high weeds and trees on either side.

"A place Brother and I come to sometime," he said. "Have you been here before?"

"I've passed it."

"Don't go into such places?"

"I'm sure it's all right."

"There are nicer places in Baton Rouge. Some pretty nice places there."

"Been going to Baton Rouge much?" she asked him.

"Not too much," he said. "I've been there two or three times. And you?"

"It's been a while."

"Maybe we'll go one day?" he said, looking at her briefly, and then out on the road again.

She did not answer him. She felt afraid being with him, and yet she wanted to be with him very much. She sat away from him, as far from him as she could get; yet, she wanted to be right up against him, feeling his arm around her. She thought about the ones at home, and yet, she did not want to think about them at all. She was sure that Raoul had left the porch by now. Where was he? Had he gone to the crib? Was he in the kitchen making coffee? Had he gone across the field with the gun? And where was Della? She would probably sit on the porch a few minutes longer and then leave also. And Lillian would still be lying across the bed with her book— half reading, half thinking, half listening.

Jackson drove off the road and parked in front of the club. It was a very small club with advertise-ments of cigarettes, soft drinks, and beer nailed against the wall. There were two small, neat white houses to the right of the club, and one, just as small, just as neat, and just as white, across the road from it. The swamps came up within a hundred yards to the left and back of the club.

Jackson and Catherine went inside. Within seemed even smaller. Five tables and a record player filled the entertainment section of the club. There was a small clean bar, and behind the bar was a fat dark woman in a green dress. The woman spoke to them as they came in. After they had sat down, the woman came up to the table to see what they wanted.

"Two beers—please."

Three other people were in the place—two men and a woman. They looked at Catherine and Jackson when they came in, and started talking again.

The woman brought the beer, and Jackson paid her.

"Aren't you one of the Carmier girls?" the woman asked Catherine.

"Yes," Catherine said.

"I thought so," the woman said. "But hasn't it been hot, though?"

"It's been murder," Catherine said.

"You not just saying it," the woman said, and left the table.

"You think we shouldn't have come?" Jackson asked.

"I'm sure it's all right," Catherine said. "She recognized me and thought she would ask. She goes to the Catholic church in Bayonne."

"Do you still go to church?" Jackson asked.

"Yes. Often as I can. Don't you?"

"Afraid not."

"You used to go all the time—you and Miss Charlotte."

"Yes, I know."

She looked across the table at him, and she did not like the way she was feeling about him. They were silent a long time, and it was uncomfortable for both of them.

"Would you like to dance?" Jackson asked.

Catherine nodded.

"I'm not good at it," Jackson said. "Warning you before we start."

She watched him go over to the record player and select a record. He came back to the table and led her out on the floor. The tempo of the music was slow, but she would not get too close to him. She did not want to feel his arms too tight around her; she did not want him to hear the beating of her heart.

The record ended almost as soon as it had begun. They went back to the table and sat down. They could not think of anything to talk about. It was an awful strain for both of them. He asked her to dance again.

She danced closer to him this time. She could feel his body hard and strong against her. It was a frightening feeling—a feeling she had never experienced before. She had danced with many men, but none had made her feel this way. Not even Bernard, her child's father, had given her this feeling. She

wanted to get away from Jackson, yet, she wanted
him to hold her closer. She wanted the record to
hurry and end, and at the same time she wanted it to
play on forever. Her hair brushed against his face.
He looked at her and smiled. She wanted to smile
back, but she was afraid to do so.

The record ended. She turned away, anxious to
get back to the table. But after she had sat down, she
wished she was dancing again.

"Another beer?" he asked her.

"Might be able to drink a half of one."

"Two," Jackson said to the woman behind the
bar.

The woman brought him the beer and he paid
and she left them.

"What should we drink to?" he asked.

She shrugged her shoulders.

"Well, let's just drink to us," he said.

They touched glasses and drank. She looked
across the table at him. She tried to make it seem
casual, but she was looking at him as she had looked
at Raoul the night before. He looked toward the bar
as Raoul had looked outside, squinted his eyes a
little as Raoul had done. He seemed to have forgotten her for a minute, then remembered she was
there, and looked at her and smiled.

"Ready to leave?" he asked.

"When you are," she said.

They went out. She went to the driver's side of
the car, and he opened and closed the door for her.
He went to the other side to get in. When she tried
to insert the key into the switch, she found that her

hand was trembling too much to do so. She knew he was looking at her. She knew he could see her trembling hand, he could hear the violent thumping of her heart. Insert the key, insert the key, she told herself. But the key slipped out of her hand down to the floor. She did not lean over to pick it up. His eyes were still on her, she could feel them. She raised her head slowly—not wanting to, but being unable to do anything else. He was already beside her. His arms were already pulling her close. Yes, she thought. Yes, darling, please kiss me, kiss me.

"Tomorrow night?" he asked her.

They were going back.

"I don't know. I'll have to see."

"I'll be waiting."

"I can't promise anything."

"You'll try?"

"Yes. I'll try."

When she turned off the highway to go into the quarters, she stopped the car and turned out the lights.

"Yes, it's best to get out here," he said.

They were looking at each other. He moved closer and kissed her. But she did not kiss him the way she had done only a few minutes ago.

"Tomorrow?" he asked her again.

She nodded, without saying anything. He got out of the car, and she drove away. When she came up to the house, she noticed a light on in Lillian's room. The rest of the house was in darkness. Then as she drove across the yard, she saw a light on in the crib.

She parked the car and went over there.

"Made it back?" Raoul said.

"Yes."

Raoul stood in the door with a pitchfork, looking back into the crib. He had begun to sweat, and Catherine could smell the sweat in his clothes mixed with the hot dry odor of the corn and shuck in the crib.

"Raking some of this old corn to the front," he said.

"Going to start pulling tomorrow?"

"Day after more likely," he said.

"Need any help?" Catherine asked.

"In that dress?" Raoul said, looking at her. "You can finish it up tomorrow if you want to. If you don't, just leave it there."

"I'll get it."

Raoul turned his back on her and looked thoughtfully at the pile of corn in front of him. After a while he leaned the fork against the wall and moved farther into the crib. Catherine saw the light moving as Raoul unhooked the lantern from against the wall and came back to the door. She reached for the lantern, but Raoul did not pass it to her.

"I can manage it," he said. "I'm not that old yet."

After stepping down to the ground and locking the door, the two of them went across the yard together. Catherine dropped back a step. She wanted to look at him again. If she looked at him and tried to reason with herself, she would not feel so much like a bitch. But as soon as she had dropped back, he became aware of it and began to shorten his stride so she would catch up again. It was something done unconsciously, but naturally. She came up even with him. She felt a desperate urge to take his hand. She had done that often when she was a little girl. She had done it even after she had grown up—whenever she felt troubled or thought he was troubled about something. But he might become suspicious if she did it tonight. He might have become suspicious already when she reached for the lantern.

He opened the gate and they went into the small yard, then into the house. She wanted to stay in the kitchen a minute with him, but she changed her mind and went up the hall to her room. Nelson was not in the bed, and she went across the hall to get him. Della was sitting in the dark by the window. The piece of white cloth she used for fanning away mosquitoes was thrown over her shoulder.

"He's asleep?" Catherine asked.

Della did not answer, she would not even look at her. Catherine picked the baby up from the bed and went out of the room. After laying him down again, she sat before the dresser and looked at herself in the mirror. I feel like a bitch, she thought. I feel like a selfish and unclean bitch. I won't see him again. That's the only answer. But the following night they lay together in a rooming house in Baton Rouge.

CHAPTER THIRTY-ONE

How had she gotten there? Everything had happened so fast. After supper, Raoul said he was going hunting. She knew when he left the house, he would be gone for three or four hours. She had driven the car out of the yard less than half an hour later. She had not wanted to leave the house that night—she had not wanted to see Jackson again. But something—how could she ever explain it? how?—had made her tell Della she was going for a ride in the car. After she had said it, she still would not leave the house for a while. Then as she came out of the yard, she saw him waiting for her. He got under the steering wheel and turned the car toward Baton Rouge. They had gone to a night club and had drunk whiskey and danced. They had danced close together, and they had looked at each other all the time that they were dancing.

Love me? he asked with his eyes.

Yes, she said with her eyes.

They had danced very slowly and close, and she could feel the whiskey making her giddy.

If I wanted you very much? he said with his eyes. If I wanted you more than anything . . . ?

Yes, she had said with her eyes. Yes.

They had danced very slowly and close and she had laid her head on his shoulder. Then they had gone back to the table and sat down, and they had looked questioningly across the table at each other. Then he had gone over to the bar and begun talking with a man. The man had looked twice over his shoulder at her—not the way most men look at you, but the way a few can—tenderly, understanding. She had not known what they were talking about at the bar until later, and when she found out she was not embarrassed or angry. When they were leaving, the man had looked at her and nodded as you might nod to a young bride, and outside she had told Jackson that she thought the man was very nice.

"He thinks you're very beautiful. He asked me why did we have to go to a place to be with each other."

"Is that what you all were talking about?"

"Yes."

"What did you tell him?"

"We had no place else to go."

"He was very nice."

They had gotten into the car and driven away, and the woman who met them at the door had not asked any unnecessary questions, but had led them down the hall to the room. She had never been inside one of these rooms, but it looked no different from any other. It was the way you came there and the way you left which made all the difference.

He lay on his side, propped up by one arm, looking down at her. She raised her hand and passed it over his face. Everything had gone so well; everything had gone so very well. And I won't ever be with you again, she thought. This is our first and last time. Never again. He leaned forward and kissed her. It was light and tender.

"What is the matter?"

She was crying.

"Nothing."

"No, what's the matter?"

"Nothing."

He lay on his side, looking down at her.

"My life?" he whispered. "Are you my life?"

He was both anxious and afraid to know the answer.

"Don't answer now," he said. "Take your time." Then he said, "I'll give you a minute."

A weary little smile came on her face. He kissed her again.

I will never see you after tonight, she thought.

"Have you ever been surrounded by a brick wall?" he asked her. "One where there's no light at all? No kind of light?"

"No."

"I was before I met you."

She looked at him a moment, and looked away. He knew what she was thinking about, and he turned her face to him again.

"Yes," he said. "I was surrounded by a brick wall. It was over my head. In order to see anything at all, I had to stand on tiptoe, to strain. Do you understand what I'm saying?"

She did not. She did not want to understand. But she told him she did.

"You're like the light. Your hair, your face; your

smile, your body. You're light. You're life."

Her hand brushed against his chin, but she drew it away quickly.

"I don't want to give up, do you understand? I don't want to ever give up! There are so many people who have gone up there—who have come from all over the world up there—and not being able to find what was promised them, they've given up. I don't want to be one of those people."

He lay beside her, his face in the pillow against her hair.

"I saw the wall rising, but I fought it. But it kept rising, kept rising, and still I fought it. So many times, I almost gave up. So many times. But I kept fighting it. That's why I left, that's why I came here. I had to get away—at least for a while. I don't believe in being walled in. I don't believe in it. I'd rather die than to live in hatred and fear. Do you know what I mean?" He raised up on his arm and looked at her. She was crying bitterly. "What's the matter? What's the matter?" But she could not control her tears.

He took her in his arms and passed his hand over her face.

"Please don't, Cathy. Please don't."

She cried harder, and he held her close and kissed her hair. Then she turned to him, pleading—but pleading what for? To be loved, kissed, to be taken? Or was she pleading for him to leave her, to never see her again? He brought her closer and kissed her hard on the mouth, and she clung to him with the desperation of a person drowning. Yet at the next moment she was pushing him away, and at the same time, hoping that he would never leave.

CHAPTER THIRTY-TWO

She must go to him again. She must feel his kisses again. She must feel his hand on her body again. She wanted to feel the muscles in his strong hard back as he lay heavily upon her.

Catherine sat at the window, looking out into the yard. It was the next day—the sun was going down, and the sound of insects filled the hot, dusty air. She was waiting for Raoul to come home so they would eat and then she would leave. But it seemed that today, of all days, Raoul was taking longer to come from the field. She wanted to go into the kitchen, but she knew how Della would look at her—at the unclean bitch that she was. But was she? The man at the bar had not thought so. The man at the bar had understood and had said yes.

The sun slipped farther and farther behind the trees, then it was completely gone. Raoul still had not come in. She strained her ears, listening for the tractor. Nothing. Dusk had set in now. Fireflies filled the air; still no Raoul. She wondered—she stood up; maybe something had happened to him. Maybe he was hurt, suffering back there alone. He would not call for help to black or white. He was

too proud for that. She started walking the floor.
Maybe something was wrong—then maybe not. She
went to the window and listened for the tractor.
Nothing. She turned from the window, biting her
finger and walking the floor. She went back to the
window again—nothing. She ran out of the room.
Della was sitting at the table when she came into the
kitchen.

"I'm going in the field," she said to Della. "Daddy
should have been home by now."

"Don't tell me you thinking 'bout him—"

She did not hear it all. She ran across the yard and
got into the car. The people moved into the ditch as
she sped through the quarters. She did not see them;
she did not think about the dust she sent flying all
over the yard and into the houses.

She did not slow up to go across the railroad, and
she could feel the bottom of the car hit against one
of the rails. She drove faster. Rows of corn, cane,
cotton shot by her like spokes in a spinning wheel.
A tree appeared—disappeared; a ditch, a bush, then
it was all behind her. But she still had far to go. He
had none of the land near the front. No, that would
have been too good for a nigger. They had put him
back near the swamps, but even back there he had
proved himself a better man than any two of them.
She had heard him say many times that if he had one
man to stand beside him stride for stride he would
raise as much crop as those five cousins all together.
"What about me?" she had said. "I can do anything
any of the others can do." He had not said anything.
He had only looked at her. He loved her, she knew

that, but at moments like those, she had the feeling that he wished she were a man instead of a woman.

She was coming up to his field, now, but she was not there yet. The car lights flashed on yellow ripe corn on either side of the road, then on tall green stalks of sugar cane that leaned toward the road like willow branches. A moment later she was passing cotton, and she noticed how much the cotton had opened during the last two weeks. She dreaded the thought that within a few days she would have to hang a sack on her shoulder, drag it from morning till night, from one end of this field to the other. She turned left, then she saw him. No, not him—the mules and the wagon. They were in a cornfield to her right. A lantern was hanging on the back of the wagon, and he was behind the wagon, too, somewhere. She heard him tell the mules go up, then stop; then go up, and stop again. She got out of the car and moved to the end of the row to wait for him. She was crying.

Just before reaching the headland where she was standing, Raoul came to the side of the wagon to turn down another row. Catherine ran toward him, crying.

"Daddy, what are you doing out here? What are you doing out here?"

"Hey, what's the matter?" he said. "What's all this for?"

She drew back and looked at him.

"I thought you were hurt."

"I'm pulling corn," he said. "Who's going to do it if I don't?"

She stood on tiptoe and kissed him.

"Hey," he said. "Cut that out now. What's the matter with you?" But he liked what she had done, and he was laughing as he said it.

"What's all this about?" he said. "That dance?"

"Daddy?"

"Is that it?"

"Yes," she said. "Yes."

"Well, you don't have to worry," he said. "You're going."

She looked up at him, loving him, admiring him, thinking: No, no, I will never go to him again, never go against you again.

"You better get on back to the front," he said. "I'll soon be coming in."

"Don't you want me to guide them for you?"

"Them?" he said. "They know these damn rows better than I do. What the world is that you got on?"

"Daddy, you know you bought me that perfume," she said, happy to be near him.

"Well, it smells all right," he said. "But don't think I'm going to be saying it too often. I hate complimenting women."

"Oh, Daddy," she said, loving him very much. "You know you're not so tough."

"Who the world you wearing that stuff for—these bullfrogs back here?"

"Daddy, you can't hurt me," she said, loving him as much as she had ever loved Jackson.

He smiled at her.

"Maybe I have a boyfriend," she said. "You ever

thought about that?"

"You going to have lot more boyfriends than you barking for," he said, "once these rattlesnakes get a whiff of that scent."

Catherine looked down at the ground at the broken-down corn stalks and weeds around her. There was not a clean space of ground anywhere in sight.

"You better go on back," Raoul said.

"Can't I do anything?"

"Not in those clothes."

She turned away from him. She was near the car when she stopped and looked at him again. He had not moved, still watching her. She ran back to him.

"Oh, Daddy," she said, laying her head on his chest. "Oh, Daddy. Do you love me, Daddy? Do you love me?" He held her close and awkwardly. "I love you so much, Daddy. I love you so much."

Then she jerked away and ran toward the car.

CHAPTER THIRTY-THREE

Jackson was waiting for Catherine on the highway. He had gone out there when he saw the car coming out of the yard. Then the car had turned left. He could see the small red light on the back get dimmer and dimmer as the car went farther into the quarters. He wondered if anything had happened. Why

would she be going into the fields this time of night? He would stay out there until she came back.

He started thinking about their being together. This was all he could think about. This was all he had been thinking about. In his room, or on the porch, or at Madame Bayonne's—he wished for the night to hurry up and come. Madame Bayonne had noticed it in his face the first day and had warned him again—but what did he care about Raoul, his aunt, or anyone else but her? Then the night would come and they would be together. Only the night would end just as fast, and they would be separated again. He would have to wait now for another night—wait, wait, wait. Would she come to him— what would he do if she did not? He did not think about this too often. He could not bear to think about it.

He looked down the quarters again. He did not see the car. He wanted to go to the store to get a bag of candies, but he was afraid she might come out there and not see him. No, he would wait. He would get her a bag of candies somewhere else. He would probably buy her a doll. He had thought about it all day. He would find an excuse to go into a store, buy the doll, have it wrapped and tied with a ribbon, and then he would give it to her.

He looked down the quarters again—nothing. Maybe he would have time to get the candy. He ran over to the store. The store was filled with people— Negroes and Cajuns alike. He could feel them looking at him as he came in. One of the Cajuns said in Creole, "I see the professor is still with us, hanh?"

No one else said anything. After paying for the bag of candies, he went out. He felt better as he walked back toward the road.

He saw the car coming in from the field; his heart beat faster in him. Then the car turned into the yard. She'll have to go in first, he thought. He waited.

He heard people talking to his right. The store had closed for the night, and the people were going home. They looked at him as they went by, but none of them said anything to him. What did he care? His mind was on Catherine. He waited. How long? Two hours? three?

The following night he waited for her again. He had the bag of candies with him again. After the store closed for the night, the people passed by him and did not speak as they had not spoken to him the night before. He waited. He waited again the night afterward. No Catherine. What had happened? Had Raoul found out? And if he had found out, why hadn't she let him know? Madame Bayonne saw it in his face. "No, he hasn't found out," she said. "If he had, you would've been one of the first to know about it. But didn't I warn you—didn't I?"

He began to think about other things now. Maybe she was right. Maybe he should forget all about it. Wasn't his life complicated enough already? He had come here to straighten out his life, not to get more involved. Wouldn't she complicate things more? But a moment later he thought about her more than ever, and that night he went to the

front to wait for her again. Nothing. He went through the quarters. Nothing. Just the old house—big, ugly, black behind the trees, and that was all.

He was sitting in the swing the next evening when Charlotte and Mary Louise came out on the porch. Charlotte did not look at him. No, she did not know what was going on, but she had quit talking to him long ago. She cooked his food and left it on the stove for him. She washed his clothes if he put them where she could find them. If he did not, then let him wash them himself. She kept away from him as he kept away from her.

Mary Louise was the same as always, but he had changed toward her. He seldom talked to her now, and when he saw her coming to the house he went to his room. He did not like the way he was acting with her, but what else could he do? It was impossible to disguise his feeling for Catherine around anyone, and it would have been much harder to try to hide it in front of Mary Louise.

"Y'all going somewhere tonight?" she asked.

He looked at her. What was she talking about?

"You and Brother?"

"No, I don't think so," he said.

She smiled at him and went out of the yard. He watched her running to catch up with Charlotte.

Jackson waited until he was sure they had gotten to the church; then he left the house. It was Della who opened the door when he knocked.

"Jackson?"

He nodded.

She was surprised to find him there; then she seemed afraid, then happy.

"Come in. Come in."

He went into the room. She pulled his head down to her and kissed him very hard, then she pushed him away to look at him better.

"But you grown; you a big man now."

"You look very well yourself, Mrs. Della."

"Shucks now, get away from here," she said, and laughed.

He smiled at her, and she smiled back, lovingly and thoughtfully. Then she seemed frightened again.

"Jackson?" Catherine said behind him.

Jackson turned to her. But he did not see his Catherine. She was very pale, her eyes were too dark. He looked for love in her face—the love that they had shared those three nights together—but he saw hatred for him instead.

"Catherine?"

"I'm sure you two want to be alone," Della said, looking first at him, then at Catherine. Catherine would not look at her. Whatever Della wanted to say with her eyes, Catherine had seen it too many times already.

"Would you like to come into the kitchen?" Catherine said. "I was baking some tea cakes."

He followed her down a dark narrow hall to the kitchen. The kitchen was extremely hot, and he could smell the sweet cakes that were in a bowl on the table.

"Care for a few of them?" she asked. She was

already getting them for him.

"Thanks."

"A Coke?"

"Thank you."

She put the things on the table for him, and Jackson sat down and began eating.

"How've you been?" Catherine asked from the window. She was washing dishes and looking into the yard and not at him. She had not looked at him once since coming into the kitchen.

"All right," he said, looking at her.

When she was through baking the cakes and had put them away, she asked if he would like to go to the front. They left the kitchen, and after stopping on the porch only a moment, they went out into the yard.

"Catherine, what's the matter?"

"Nothing."

He grabbed her arm and jerked her around. They were standing under one of the big oak trees to the side of the house.

"I thought we ought to stop," she said.

"What?" he said. "You thought we ought to stop?"

"You said yourself that it was all wrong. And it is wrong."

"Is it Raoul, Catherine?"

She looked down at the ground. He raised her head up roughly.

"Don't look away from me. Is it him?"

She turned her head and he turned it back and held it so she would have to look at him.

"And how about me? And how about yourself?"

She was silent, looking at him, the tears already running down her face.

"How about us?" he screamed at her. "Me and you? Don't you think we should have a chance?"

He saw that it was no use talking to her, she did not hear half of what he was saying. Her face began to shake violently in his hand. He jerked his hand away from her and she looked down at the ground.

"Is that all you wanted? Was that it? Just once in bed?"

She raised her head and looked at him. He could tell she was hurt. Not angry—hurt.

"Was that it? One hour—was that enough for you? Or should we have another hour right here so it would last you the rest of your life?"

She looked at him, the tears running down her face. She was hurt, not angry. He jerked at her.

"Come on, Catherine. One more hour. Come on. Right here on the ground."

The tears ran down her face, but she did not say anything. He pushed her away, and her back hit against the tree. He could see her face grimace with pain, but he moved toward her again. He raised her face to his.

"I ought to break your neck," he said. "I ought to break your neck."

He took his hand away from her face, and she looked down at the ground again. Suddenly there was a light across the yard. He looked toward the house. He saw Lillian standing at the window, watching them. He looked at Catherine again. He started to say something else to her, but he did not know what to say; and he turned away and walked out of the yard.

CHAPTER THIRTY-FOUR

He had to get away from here. He had to get away. He would either go mad or get into trouble if he did not get away. The first chance he got, he would tell Charlotte that he was going back. From the way she had been acting the last few days, she probably would be glad to hear it. And it would be better for everybody. Surely, it would be better for Catherine and Raoul. Then there would be nothing to stand between them. They could have each other all to themselves for the rest of their twisted lives.

He raised his head just before coming up to the gate. He saw Charlotte and Mary Louise on the porch. But why were they home so early? Church would not be over for at least two hours. Well, it was all for the better. He would tell her now and be done with it. Let her cry, let her scream at him, let her do anything she wanted to do. He would never get this chance again.

Neither Charlotte nor Mary Louise looked at him when he came into the yard. No one said anything to him when he spoke, and no one paid any attention to him when he sat on the railing at the end of the porch. There was absolute silence for a long time, and he felt as cowardly about telling her as he always had.

"I thought you were going to church," he said to Mary Louise. He would start with her first.

"Changed us mind."

"What are your two candidates going to do without you?"

"You making fun of the Lord, Jackson?" Charlotte said, turning on him.

He looked at her, but did not say anything. He would wait his chance.

"Well, not here," she said. "You don't play with Him in my house. Get out in the road if you want play with Him."

She stood up to go inside the house.

"Aunt Charlotte?" he said. She kept on walking. "Just a minute," he said. He would not hesitate another moment.

"What?" she said, stopping and looking at him. "What you said to me? I'm not one of your women, you know."

But he had not said half of what he wanted to say to her when she staggered against the door as if someone had hit her with his fist. Mary Louise jumped up from the swing to help her inside.

"No," she cried. "No. I can stand, I can stand. I got a pillar so strong to lean on nothing can drag me down." She was talking to Jackson and not to Mary Louise. "Nothing can harm me. Nothing can hurt me. Not the pillar I lean on. Not the pillar I lean on." She moved to open the screen, but she fell to the floor. Jackson left the railing and Mary Louise broke away from the swing to help her up.

"Get away from me, Jackson," she screamed at him. "Get away from me. Get away and stay away. Stay away."

"What happened?" a woman called from the gate.

"She fell," Mary Louise said. She looked around at the woman who had already pushed the gate open and was coming into the yard. "Miss Selina . . ."

The woman ran up on the porch and she and Mary Louise got Charlotte to her feet. When Jackson tried to open the door for them, Selina told him to get away.

She and Mary Louise helped Charlotte inside and laid her across the bed. Selina told Mary Louise to get a pan of cold water, and while Mary Louise was in the kitchen, Selina went to the dresser and began searching in one of the drawers.

"Can I help you find something?" Jackson asked.

"Ain't you done done enough helping for one day?"

"All I did was tell her I was going back."

"Good," the woman said. "Good. 'Cause if you don't go back, you go'n kill her, or Raoul go'n kill you."

She found a towel in one of the drawers and came back to the bed. Mary Louise met her at the foot of the bed with the pan of water. After soaking the towel in the water and wringing it half dry, Selina passed the towel over Charlotte's face. Jackson stood by the mantelpiece watching her.

"How you feel?" Selina asked.

"I'm all right," Charlotte said.

"You sure you don't need a doctor, Miss Charlotte?"

"I'm all right," Charlotte said. "Just got little dizzy there, that's all."

Selina continued to pass the towel over her face. Mary Louise stood at the foot of the bed holding the pan of water and crying.

"You can go throw that out," Selina said. Mary Louise did not move. She stood by the bed looking at Charlotte as though she were in a trance. "Mary Louise?" the woman said, looking over her shoulder at her.

Mary Louise turned with the pan of water and went back into the kitchen. Jackson heard the water hit the ground, and heard Mary Louise hanging the pan against the wall again.

"You can go out," Selina said to Mary Louise when she came back into the bedroom. "And take him out of here."

"Who the hell are you supposed to be?" Jackson said to the woman.

"Mary Louise, would you please get that boy out of here?" the woman said.

Mary Louise touched Jackson timidly on the arm and nodded toward the door. He did not move. She pulled on his arm this time, but as timidly as she had touched him. "Come on," she said. Still he hesitated a moment before following her outside. The woman on the bed had not taken her eyes off him all the time he was standing there—looking at him as though she was ready to throw him out bodily if Mary Louise could not do it by talking to him.

"I don't know why the hell I came back here in the first damn place," he said. "I swear to God I don't."

"Miss Charlotte, Jackson," Mary Louise whispered, so he would keep his voice down.

"She saw us?" he asked Mary Louise when they were on the porch. "Was that it?"

"She saw y'all," Mary Louise said.

He looked at her. How could she see him, when she had left for church a full half hour before he left the house.

"We was out there talking to Miss Jane Burke when Miss Jane Burke seen you go in the yard. She told Miss Charlotte, and Miss Charlotte came on back to the house. I came back with her."

CHAPTER THIRTY-FIVE

Brother came up to the house about an hour later and asked Jackson if he wanted to go as far as Bayonne. Jackson told him that Charlotte was ill, but that was all Jackson said. Brother went inside the house, returned a few minutes later, and sat on the railing of the porch. Mary Louise had to explain everything else about Charlotte to him.

When Selina got ready to leave, she told them that the only thing troubling Charlotte was that she needed rest. Mary Louise said that she would stay there the remainder of the night. Selina said it was not necessary since Charlotte was already asleep. Mary Louise insisted that she would stay. Selina said that she would be back tomorrow morning and she told everyone good night. Brother and Mary Louise told her good night, and Mary Louise went inside to sit by the bed. Brother and Jackson remained on the porch talking. Around two o'clock Brother went home, leaving Jackson alone on the porch.

"You ought to go to bed," Mary Louise said at the door.

"I'm not sleepy; I'll probably be up all night anyhow. Why don't you go?"

Mary Louise came outside and sat in the swing beside him.

"How is she?"

"Resting."

Jackson looked at Mary Louise sitting beside him. Her hands were clasped together and she was looking down at the floor. It seemed that it had been a long, long time since they had been alone together.

"I'm sorry, Mary Louise."

"You had to tell her one day," she said. "What's the matter? You and Catherine had a fight?"

"Why do you say that?"

"You look mad when you came home."

"I guess we did."

"I guess that's how it is when you in love."

"She loves Raoul, not me."

"She love you," Mary Louise said. "And you love her." He looked at her. "Yeah, you love her, Jackson. You love her."

They were together about an hour, then she went inside to sit beside the bed. He was alone again.

Why had he made such a fool of himself these last few days? He knew in the beginning it would not work out. What could she do for him? Get in his way, slow him down, stop him from searching, and that was all. He was glad that it was over with. Mary Louise had said he still loved Catherine, but he would show her that she was wrong.

Jackson got up and went inside. Mary Louise sat beside the bed asleep. He looked at his aunt and looked at Mary Louise again. Both of them were snoring.

He went into his room and came back with his coat and spread it over Mary Louise's shoulders. Mary Louise did not know anything about it. He looked at his aunt again, and for a moment, he had the feeling that she was dead. He became so frightened that he was unable to move. He checked himself quickly and went out of the room. He told himself again that he had to get out of this place or he would go insane.

The next day Jackson tried every way he knew to be helpful around the house, but the woman who had helped Charlotte to bed the night before ignored every effort he made. After bathing and feeding her patient—two things Charlotte would much rather have done herself—Selina went to the store to get something for dinner. Then, while her dinner was cooking on the stove, she swept and scrubbed the entire house—including the front and back porches. Jackson asked several times if he could be of any help to her, but each time he asked, Selina pretended that she had not heard. Around noon she told him that his food was ready if he cared to eat, but he had better mind how he went across the floor. Charlotte was asleep and she did not want her disturbed. Jackson did as he was told, wishing to get on the better side of the woman, but the woman had no more to say to him the rest of the day. When Mary Louise came from work that afternoon, she and Mary Louise talked a few minutes, then she left the house.

"Reckoned y'all didn't get along too killing good today?" Mary Louise said.

"Not too killing good," Jackson agreed.

Mary Louise smiled and looked at him as though she understood him quite well now and wondered why the others did not. After looking in at Charlotte, who was asleep, Mary Louise said that she would have to go home, but she would return in a few minutes. Jackson followed her out to the front porch.

"See you been reading?" she said, nodding toward the yellow paperback book in the swing.

"Tried to," Jackson said. "Didn't get too much of it done."

"What is it? A story?"

"Greek poetry," he said.

She looked at the book a long time, as though she

were trying to figure out the words. She had no idea what any word meant, and she looked at him and smiled. He smiled back, assuring her that it really did not matter. She left the house.

"Selina?" he heard Charlotte calling from the room. He went in to see what she wanted.

"She's gone," Jackson said. "Can I help you, Aunt Charlotte?"

Charlotte looked at him sympathetically. She did not like the way both she and the other woman were treating him, but, still, she was not ready to forgive him for going back. She shook her head.

"Mary Louise was at the house," he said. "She'll be back in a few minutes."

"Mary Louise done—" but she did not say any more. It would have given him a reason to say something else, and she wanted him to believe that she still felt the same way as she did the day before.

Charlotte did and she did not. She did not think for a moment that he had the right to go back. She had sacrificed too much of herself for him. She had hoped, prayed, waited too long for him to come back just to see him turn around and leave her like this. What was she going to do after he was gone? What would her life be like after he was gone? All of her dreams, her hopes were wrapped up in the day that he would come back to her.

Even so, she did not approve of what she and the other woman were doing to him. This was his home and he should be treated as though it was his home. Yet, didn't she have the right to show how she felt?

Not only did she have the right, but what else could she do? Her life for the future was total darkness now—what else could she do?

Charlotte had been thinking about this all morning, and the harder she tried to reach an answer, the more confused and frustrated she became.

Jackson could tell by Charlotte's face that he could not be of any help, and he nodded and went out on the porch again.

Two women came up to the house and asked about Miss Charlotte. Jackson nodded toward the door, and the women went inside. People had been coming up to the house like that all day, but Selina had turned most of them back. Charlotte needed rest, she told them, and the only way she could get her proper rest was to be left alone. Most everyone agreed that Selina was right and left the house immediately. But as soon as one group had gone, another group would show up.

Each person who came there blamed Jackson for Charlotte's illness. They either accused him by the way they looked at him, or by the way they spoke a few words to each other about him—which he could not help overhearing. Jackson became angry at first and tried to stare at whoever looked toward him in the swing, but he gave it up after telling himself that he was too intelligent a person to play games like these. He knew he was innocent, he would let them stare all they wanted, he would get a book to read.

A little old woman—somewhere between eighty and ninety—in a long gingham dress, carrying a walking cane, and smoking a corncob pipe that was so old it had nearly become the same color she was, changed his attitude completely. After threatening to beat Selina with her walking cane when Selina told her she could not see Charlotte because Charlotte was asleep, the old woman tore into the bedroom and remained beside the bed almost two hours. When she got ready to leave, she walked up to Jackson in the swing and told him if anything happened to Charlotte he would have no one but himself to blame. He tried to ignore the old woman just as he had done the others, but she stood before him (she was so close that he could almost feel the pipe in his face) until he raised his head.

"Yes," she said, "you. Yes, you."

They continued to stare at each other, but he knew if he stared at her until Doomsday he would never be able to stare her down. Neither would he be able to explain to her if he tried. They were like trees, like rocks, like the ocean, these old people. Never understanding, never giving.

He looked down at the floor, and a moment later, though he did not hear her leaving, he felt that she had gone. He raised his head to watch her go down the quarters.

"I am guilty," he thought. "Yes, yes, I am. I was born guilty. But guilty or no guilty, I'm going back. And with time I will forget every bit of it. The whole lot . . ."

CHAPTER THIRTY-SIX

When Mary Louise came back to the house, Jackson told her he was going for a walk. He did not want to be near her, because she would remind him of everything. She did not mean any harm—he knew that—but just being near her would remind him of the fool he had made of himself with Catherine. He would be conscious every moment of the sorrow he had caused his aunt. Before leaving the house, he asked Mary Louise if she needed anything. She shook her head.

Once Jackson was in the road, he did not know which way to turn. He would have liked to go for a walk across the field, but then he would have had to pass that damned house to get back there. And then after he had passed the house he would be stared at by everyone else in the quarters. No, he had better not go that way. It was too hot to be bothered, and he might have said something to someone. He started toward the highway.

I have to get the hell out of this place, he was thinking. I have to get out of here as soon as possible. I'll wait until she's up, I'll make up to her in some kind of way, and then I'm going to get the hell out of here.

But where to? Back to San Francisco? Then what? What then? I came here because I had to get away from there a while. Am I going back to the same thing? But if not to San Francisco, then where to?

He was on the highway. He stood there awhile, not knowing which way to turn. He looked at the old cypress tree down the riverbank. Gray-black Spanish moss hung from every limb like long, ugly curtains. Jackson felt as though these curtains hung over his heart.

He turned away, looking up the highway, then down. Hot gray asphalt stretched in either direction as far as the eyes could see. He thought he saw Brother's car parked in front of the store, and he took a better look. It was Brother's car and he started over there.

Jackson could see Brother standing on the porch, talking with several other people. Brother was facing the other way, but someone must have mentioned Jackson's name, and Brother looked around just as he was coming up the steps.

"Taking a stroll?" Brother asked.

"Thought I would. Just getting in from Bay-onne?"

"Few minutes," Brother said.

Jackson looked at the people whom Brother had been talking to, but did not say anything to them. No one spoke to him, either.

"Getting a Coke," he said to Brother. "Can I get you one?"

"How about a beer?" Brother said. "On me."

"Maybe some other time."

He wanted a beer. He needed one badly. But he would have to go to a sideroom to get it. The storekeeper sold beer to whites inside the store, but not to Negroes. Negroes could buy and drink theirs in a small room to the side. Jackson had not gone to the sideroom since coming there.

He went into the store and came out a minute later with two bottles of Coca-Cola. He gave Brother one of the bottles, and he leaned against a post, drinking from the other one. The Negroes who had been talking to Brother had become silent. Two Cajuns at the far end of the porch were also silent and were looking at him.

Jackson drank from his Coca-Cola bottle and looked out at the river. A sailboat halfway out was drifting leisurely toward Bayonne. Jackson could see that the people on the boat were white. They were diving off the boat, swimming away from it, then back to the boat again. Jackson watched them a while, and looked away. What a place to be in. Nothing to do and nowhere to go—unless you wanted to go to a sideroom for a bottle of beer.

He knew that the people on the porch were looking at him. But what did he care? It gave him a sense of importance to know they were concerned about him. He turned his head to the side. The Cajuns quickly looked away. He almost laughed. What fools. Just because he did not clown in front of them and drink in the sideroom with the other Negroes, they were suspicious of him. Already he had heard that they were asking whether or not he was a Freedom Rider. What a joke. He a Freedom Rider? And what would he try to integrate, this stupid grocery store? He felt like laughing in their stupid faces.

He drank from the bottle. The Negroes were also looking at him. He could tell without turning around. No, they were no better than the Cajuns. Just as bad. Behind his back they called him "Mr. Stuck-up." He was not "Mr. Stuck-up"; he could not think of anything to talk with them about, and drinking in that sideroom was out of the question. He would never go in there. Let them call him what they wanted.

He drank the last of his Coca-Cola and took the empty bottle back inside. He had just come out on the porch again when he saw Catherine driving up in front of the store. Raoul was in the car with her. Catherine stopped at the gas pump, and Raoul got out of the car and looked toward the store.

"Gas?" Claude asked him.

"Yes," Raoul said.

While Claude put gas in the car, Raoul got the air hose and began checking each tire.

For a while Jackson would not look at Catherine. He knew if he had, he would have gone out there, jerked her out of the car, and knocked her to the ground. He felt like calling her all the dirty names he ever heard anyone call a woman. He wanted to tell everyone out there that she was Raoul's lover.

But when he did look at her, he felt none of this. It was like dropping a piece of ice on a hot stove. All hatred toward her melted—he loved her more now than ever. She was also looking at him, but he could

not believe what she was saying to him with her
eyes. How could he believe her after what had
happened last night? What are you trying to do,
make me jump on Raoul? he asked her. Is that what
you want? Is that what you're asking me to do? No,
she said; that isn't what I want. Can't you understand? Look around you—look at those around
you; can't you understand? They continued to look
at each other a while, then she looked away a
moment, then at him again.

Jackson looked at Raoul. Raoul was squatting
down beside the tire with his back toward the store.
Jackson looked at Raoul's strong, hard back. He
could see the shoulder muscles bulge out under the
thin blue shirt that Raoul wore. This was the nearest
that Jackson had been to Raoul, but he found
himself not hating him. He knew he should—he had
been brought up to hate the man—but seeing him
this close for the first time, he found himself unable
to do so. But why? Was it because of the others
who hated him, and he could not possibly agree
with them on anything? Was that it? What other
reason could it be? After all, Raoul stood beween
him and what he wanted most. He had all the
reasons in the world to hate him.

But he did not hate Raoul. Instead, he admired
him. There was something about the man, different
from all the others around there. What was it? Yes,
he knew. He was still trying to stand when all the
odds were against him. That was it, that was the
only thing. He liked that in people, he liked that in
anyone. So that's why she went back to him. Was

that it? Was that it? That must have been it. Raoul couldn't possibly love her as much as he, Jackson, did. It must have been that. It must have been the odds against him that brought her back to him. He looked at her again. Is that why you went back to him—because he's alone? What about me? Am I not as alone as he? She looked away a moment, then at him again. Say it's over between us, he said. Say it's over with. But she looked away again.

Raoul finished checking the tires at about the same time that the storekeeper finished putting gas in the car. The two men went inside the store. Raoul did not say anything to anyone when he went in or when he came back out. Jackson watched him get into the car beside Catherine and pass her a small package that looked like a bar of candy. Catherine smiled, glanced quickly at Jackson, and backed the car away from the store.

There was silence. There had been silence all the time that Raoul and Catherine were out there. And even after they had gone, there was silence still. The men wanted to talk, but they could not begin yet. One other person had to leave. When Jackson walked away, one of the Negroes said:

"You watch something."

They could see him going up the road. He was walking between the highway and the riverbank.

"Don't say nothing," one of the other Negroes said.

"His aunt sick there now, you know," the first one said. "And for that same reason—him and her, there."

"I'll tell you one thing," the storekeeper said. "If Raoul ever get hold of it . . ."

The storekeeper had said this to keep the Negroes talking.

"Don't say nothing," one of the Negroes said, falling into the trap. "I bound you it'ud be something."

The two Cajuns at the far end of the porch looked at each other. One nodded to the other, and they moved closer to where the Negroes were talking.

Brother thought he had heard enough, and he went down the steps and got into his car. He did not like it at all about Jackson's going into the yard yesterday—he had not heard about it until this morning. When Mary Louise was telling him about Charlotte last night, she had not mentioned anything about Catherine and Jackson. She had only said that Jackson had told Charlotte that he was going back to California. But Brother was not going to stay out there and listen to the Negroes and Cajuns talk about him. He knew how the Cajuns felt about Jackson and he knew how they felt about Raoul, and he knew they would keep the Negroes talking about both as long as they were out there.

When he turned off the highway into the quarters, he saw a car parked in front of Charlotte's house. He thought she might have gotten worse, and he drove faster. Before coming up to the house, he drove into the ditch and parked behind the car in front of the door. When he came into the yard, he saw Mary Louise sitting in the swing.

"Miss Charlotte—she ain't no worse?"

"Reverend Armstrong just stopped by."

He looked toward the door, but he could not see anything through the blackened screen, and he went to the swing to sit down.

"Seen Jackson?" Mary Louise asked.

"Yeah. He went walking up the road."

They were silent a moment.

"Didn't Catherine come out there?" Mary Louise asked.

"Yeah," Brother said, not looking at her.

Mary Louise continued looking at him, but she did not ask any more questions. Brother could feel that she wanted to.

"Don't tell me you still love Jackson, Mary Louise?"

"No," she said.

Brother was looking at her now. He could tell by her eyes that she was lying.

CHAPTER THIRTY-SEVEN

Reverend Armstrong sat beside the bed with his legs crossed and his arms folded. He and Charlotte had been talking now about fifteen minutes. He had inquired about her health. Her health was all right. She was a little tired, but that was all. They had talked about the weather. The weather had been very hot and dry the last few weeks, but they expected rain any day now. They had talked about the gardens. The gardens had been doing quite well under these conditions.

Charlotte knew that Reverend Armstrong had come there for more than just a casual talk, and all the time they were talking about her health, the garden, and the weather, she was anticipating the moment when he would turn to the main thing he had come there to talk about. A child returning home with a report card of nothing but D's and F's could not have dreaded this moment any more than she did.

The moment came.

"You got to put yourself in my place, Reverend," she said. "All my life I ain't never had nothing. Nothing. No kinda learning. No kinda—nothing. Worked hard all my life; and for nobody but him. Look like I got that right."

"What right is that, Sister Charlotte? Not to talk to him? Is that the right you're speaking of?"

"I helt him when he was a little baby. Next to my bosom. His mon was in the field working—cutting cane. I helt him—skinny's he could be. Holding him one hand and trying to cook with the other. I felt his little heart beat 'gainst my bosom. 'Member how he used to grab a handful of my hair—and all the time I'm trying to cook there. I just didn't born him, Reverend. That's all. I just didn't born him."

"I understand."

"Do you, Reverend? Do you understand?"

"I understand."

"Watched him grow up there—skinny's a weed.

Watched him go to school—the first one to take him to church. Saw that he got religion—baptized. Now . . ." She became quiet, crying softly to herself.

Reverend Armstrong waited patiently for a minute or two.

"I think before anything else you consider yourself a Christian, don't you, Sister?"

"Yes, sir," she said. "But I got a heart."

"Yes. I understand. But your duty as a Christian—"

"But I got a heart, Reverend, sir; I got a heart."

"I know how much you must love him. But Mary must 'a' loved Christ that much, too; don't you think so?"

She was silent.

"Don't you think so, Sister Charlotte? She loved Him?"

She was silent, crying softly. He was silent a while, too, looking at her.

"Sister Charlotte?" he said.

"Yes, sir?" she said.

"But she gave Him up. Don't you think it was a hardship for her to bear?"

"I got nothing, Reverend."

"You have Him. And when you come down to it, ain't He the only one who count?"

She was silent, crying softly.

"Sister Charlotte?"

She looked at him. "Reverend, you got two sons. You got two. How you'd feel if they was both took from you at once?"

"I would lean on Him. I would lean on Him
more."

"Reverend, look at my side."

"I am, Sister Charlotte."

"I'm a old woman. I'm old. Two more years—
three more, the most. I ain't never had a thing. Is
that too much I'm asking for?"

"Normally, I would say no. But when it starts
blocking your duty as a Christian, I have to say it is.
In this case, that's what it's doing, Sister Charlotte."

"I'm a Christian, Reverend," she said. "I can't be
nothing else but."

"I know that. I know. But the first thing a
Christian must learn is sacrifice. And to be able to
sacrifice the thing you like most is the truest test you
can have."

"Reverend, I love my boy. That's all I want in
this life, Reverend; to love him."

"To have him, Sister Charlotte. To have him."

"Yes," she said. "Yes."

"But this is not the Christian way."

"To love?"

"Not to love. To love is. But to have, to possess."

"I'll never get in his way. I just want him here
with me. I'll never get in his way."

"You can't have him here with you, Sister Charlotte. He must go back."

"And me?" she said.

"You must continue the work."

The tears ran down her face.

"Continue? And how long?"

Reverend Armstrong was stuck for an answer.

"How long, Reverend?"

"Until He calls," he said.

She looked at him a moment, and turned her head, and the tears rolled down her face.

"Look around you, Sister Charlotte. Look around you. Things ain't like they used to be. Nothing is. They ain't staying; they leaving. And the few that's here now ain't nothing like us when we was their age.

"I get up there and preach every Sunday, but I can tell. I look out there at them, and I can tell. Once there I would get out there with my fist and beat the fool out of a bunch of them. You know the old saying: 'You can't preach Heaven in them, you beat the other place out.' But it's not like that any more. No more. You got to talk now. You got to talk. You got to talk and pray and hope."

He was silent a while. His legs still crossed, his arms still folded, he was looking at her.

"There ain't but a few of us left now, Sister Charlotte. Just a few of us left. The old ones leaving us every day, the young ain't joining no more. So it's left up to us. Us few to keep it going, to keep the lamp burning till He come back. More than ever before He need us now. Nothing else is to get in the way. More than ever before we must sacrifice—willing to give up everything for Him. There's only a few of us, and us few must carry the load. Heavy? Course it's go'n be heavy. Probably heavier now than ever before. But we must keep going. Do you understand what I'm saying?"

She did not answer, crying softly.

"Sister Charlotte?"

She nodded as a child would, still crying softly.

"I know how you feel. But duty comes first. Nothing but duty. Nothing."

He touched her on the arm. Electricity ran through her as if the Lord Himself had touched her. She knew from then on her life would be devoted only to God.

She heard Jackson come into the yard. The minister had been gone now half an hour. Jackson stopped on the porch where Brother and Mary Louise were. She tried to hear whether they were saying anything. No, they were silent. He came into the room. It was dark in the room and she could hardly see his face.

"Jackson?"

He was nearly in the kitchen. He came back and stood beside the bed. She looked up at him, but she could not think of anything to say. After a while she nodded her head.

"Eat your food 'fore it get cold," she said.

CHAPTER THIRTY-EIGHT

He was not hungry at all, but the food was there, and he forced himself to eat a little of it. Then, after he had washed his plate, he went to his room and lay across the bed. It was dark in the room—warm and dark—and he lay on his back, looking up at the ceiling.

What was he going to do now that he was forgiven? She had said only a few words—"Eat your food before it gets cold—" but he knew from those few words that he was forgiven. How did it come about? What had caused it? He did not know, but what did it matter?

Well, he was forgiven. So, he was forgiven. Now what? Was he going to get up and start packing his suitcase? Or was he going to wait until tomorrow to start packing? Maybe he would wait until Saturday. But he did not like leaving a place on a weekend—so maybe he would wait until next Monday.

He did not know what he wanted to do. He knew he would leave eventually. There was nothing else he could do. But when, when all the time he knew she was still down there and that she still loved him. When would he leave?

He ought to leave now, he told himself. Hadn't that been the promise? As soon as she's well, I'm going to make it up to her some kind of way and then I'm going to get out of here, he had said. He had said that when?—only today. Only today he had said it. And wasn't that the most intelligent thing to do? Hadn't Madame Bayonne warned him about Catherine? And when he tried to show how stupid the whole idea was, wasn't it proven that she was right?

He ought to get out of here now. No, his aunt was not well and up—she would probably be in bed another couple of days. But he should get out of

here, anyhow. Mary Louise would look after his
aunt—he was sure of that; and even if he did stay,
why would he stay? For her? No; and he would be
lying to himself if he said so.

He knew he should leave without ever trying to
see Catherine again. He knew that for sure. What
good could come of it? If she said yes, I'll go with
you, then what? What then? That would mean he
would have to settle down, quit searching. But how
could he settle down—and what to? Teaching?
Teaching what? How could he teach when he did
not believe in what he was teaching? What else
could he do—get some kind of Civil Service job?
And how long would he be satisfied with that? No,
he ought to get out of here. He ought to get out of
here now.

But he did not get out, and the next few days
were miserable for him. Nothing he did worked out
for him. He tried reading a book, but he read the
same lines over and over. He tried playing solitary,
but he could not concentrate on the cards either. He
would not leave the house either day or night—
lying across the bed in broad daylight, sometimes
for hours.

Charlotte was up now and moving around. All
day long he heard her going from the kitchen to the
porch, from the porch to the kitchen. Sometimes
she would stop by his room and listen a few minutes
before going on again. When people came up to the
house and asked about him (not that they cared
anything about him, but it was the right thing to
do) she told them that he had just gone into his

room, and he was probably studying. She told them that he studied a lot—preparing himself for his teaching when he went back to California. Charlotte did not know what he was doing in the room all this time, but whatever it was, it was no business of theirs. Only to Mary Louise and sometimes to Brother would she talk about him.

"You think he sick?" she asked Mary Louise.

"I don't know."

"You think he et something?"

"I don't know."

"You think it's her? You think it's Catherine? You think that's possible?"

"I don't know," Mary Louise said.

When Brother stopped by the house—he had gone back to work now—Charlotte asked him if he knew. Brother said no'm, he did not. Then after he had gone, Jackson would hear Charlotte coming up to his door, stopping a moment, then walking by again. The only time she would dare knock and come into his room was at mealtime. While he sat at the table staring vacantly at the wall, she would take quick, furtive glances at him. Sometimes he would say something to her, sometimes he would not say a word throughout the entire meal. She would not be sitting at the table with him, but she would be in the kitchen, pretending to be busy. Once, just before going back to his room, he looked at her. He looked at her a long time—the way he might have looked at her when he was small and when he thought she was the greatest person in the world. He felt like going up to her and putting his arm around her; he felt like giving her a big kiss on the jaw and telling her that he hated himself for the way he had become. But he did none of this. He was unable to do it. But even if he could, and did, what would she think? He knew what she would think. She would try to work her way into his feeling; try to show him why he should stay here, when all the time it was impossible.

In his room, while lying across the bed, standing at the window, or sitting in the chair, he thought about all kinds of things. Why didn't he ask Catherine to leave with him—he still thought she would leave if he insisted—settle down to teaching and forget everything else? Why did he have to believe in teaching? It was a good paying job and you had three months off each year—so why believe? Why couldn't he be like the rest and go along with the game? Why worry about selling one's soul—what is a soul? Why worry about it when everyone else was doing it? He would think about something totally different. Why didn't he join the Peace Corps and get away from everything? But what would he do in the Peace Corps? Teach English? But if he taught English in the Peace Corps, why couldn't he settle down and marry and teach English? He thought about something else. He ought to join the merchant marines and go to Africa. He would probably love it in Africa. Why didn't he go into a monastery and become a priest? He wondered if committing suicide took a lot of courage.

Saturday afternoon, he was standing at the window in his room when Charlotte came in with a letter.

"For you," she said.

He took the letter. "Thanks."

"Don't you think you ought to get out sometime, Jackson?" she asked timidly.

"I'm all right," he said, and looked out of the window.

She did not like the way he looked, but she did not say any more. It had taken all of her courage to say those few words. She left the room.

He opened the envelope that she had brought him.

"Pardon me for not writing a long and formal letter. There's a dance in Bayonne Sunday night. Being held at the Catholic Hall. We'll be there. Hope you come. Lillian."

He read it again. He wondered if Catherine had gotten Lillian to write the letter. He wondered if Catherine had written it herself and had signed Lillian's name. If neither, then Lillian had done it. But why? What would she get out of it? He read it again. Maybe he had seen the wrong name at the bottom of the page. No, he had not. It was Lillian's. Beautiful penmanship—a name that had been written a million times.

What should he do? Should he go to Bayonne? He knew he should not. He knew he should get the first bus out of here. But he knew he would not do it. He knew he would go to Bayonne, to her, even if the same thing must happen all over again.

When Charlotte got ready to leave for church that evening, she called from the other side to tell him that she was going. He asked himself, shouldn't

he go to church with her. Would that be too much
for him to do? Didn't he owe her at least that much?
No, he told himself; I can't do anything that I don't
have faith in. I don't have faith in her church any
more, and I won't pretend that I do. He picked up a
book and tried to read, but that was impossible.

When Charlotte returned from church about
three hours later, he heard her walking by his door
as though she were trying to hear whether he was
still awake. Mary Louise was with her. He could
hear them talking very softly not to disturb him if
he were asleep. Mary Louise left the house, and a
few minutes later he heard his aunt saying her
prayers and getting ready for bed. He still lay wide
awake—as awake as he had been all day. He knew
he would not be able to sleep at all, and when he
thought his aunt was no longer awake, he got up
and went out into the quarters. This was the first
time he had been out of the yard since Tuesday, and
he felt as though he had been let out of a prison.

He stopped to look at the Carmiers' house when
he came up even with the gate. The house was dark
and quiet. The big oak and pecan trees surrounded
the house like sentinels. He wondered what he
would do if she suddenly came to the window. She
did not, and he went on.

The quarters were extremely quiet. There was a
moon, very high and very bright. Shadows from the
trees, from the weeds along the ditch bank, from the
old warped picket fences, lay across the road in
front of him. Every house was quiet, looking gray
and ghostlike. A dog barked at him every now and

then, but other than that, absolute silence.

He walked on in the middle of the road. The dust was cool and soft and felt good under his shoes. He crossed the railroad tracks, but did not know where to go from here. To his right was the cemetery. He could see the big trees and the high weeds that stood over each grave. He thought he would walk over there. When he came up to the fence that surrounded the cemetery, he looked through the fence at places where graves ought to be, or where he thought they had been. He could not see any graves for the high weeds, and he was not sure that he was looking in the right places. He moved along the fence, but he could not see anything. When he was a child—ten years ago—he could have found his way to any grave in the cemetery with his eyes shut. Today he did not know if he was looking into the same cemetery. He moved away from the fence, stood back, looked over everything again, and then turned away.

He did not like the way he was feeling. He was feeling empty. He did not like being empty—unable to recognize things, unable to associate himself with things. He did not like being unable to recognize the graves. He did not like being unable to associate with the people. He did not like being unable to go to church with his aunt, or to drink in the sideroom with Brother. What then? Was it to be there? No, that was not it either. If neither there nor here, neither the living nor the dead, then what?

He was in the quarters again—the shadows were all around him. The high, bright moon made the dust in the road look as white as snow.

He stopped in front of the church. This had also been his school. He went into the yard to look at his church-school. How small it seemed. How large then, but how small now. How small was the yard. He could hardly knock a ball out of here once—but look at the size of it. What had happened? Had he grown so big or had the place actually shrunk in those ten years?

He went up to one of the windows to look inside. He looked at the straightback benches upon which he had sat in church as well as in school. He looked at the places against the wall where blackboards had once hung. How many whippings he had gotten for giving the wrong answer to a problem, the wrong definition to a word. Madame Bayonne loved him —yes; but she would whip him as quickly as she would any of the others—quicker sometimes. He looked toward the front of the church where she used to sit behind her desk. It was not really a desk. It was a table—the same table that the minister and his deacons used on Sundays for fixing the sacraments. Once it seemed that the distance from the blackboard to the table was a mile; now he felt as if he could have made it within a stride or two.

He went to the back of the church and looked over the yard. A sugar-cane field came all the way up to the yard from the side and from the back. He looked at the two old toilets by the fence, and he looked at the old elm tree in the corner of the fence which had been killed by lightning even before he left. There was a pecan tree across the ditch, and he remembered how the wind and the rain used to blow the pecans into the yard, and how he and the other children used to gather them and eat them during recess. He went back there to get a better look at the tree, but after a while he turned and walked away.

Just before going out of the yard he saw something shining on the ground in front of him. When he picked it up, he saw that it was a small piece of a broken key chain. He started to throw it away, but changed his mind and put it in his pocket.

Part Three

CHAPTER THIRTY-NINE

CATHERINE wondered whether Jackson had gone back to California. Five days had gone by now and she had not caught a glimpse of him. She did not think too much of it the first day. Maybe he did not have a reason to go down the quarters the first day. And why should he pass by the house after what had happened? But when she did not see him the second day, Thursday, she began to wonder. She got into the car that afternoon and went out to the store. He was not there and neither was he sitting on the porch. Mary Louise was in the swing, but she could not tell from Mary Louise's face whether he was there or not. Later, she drove through the quarters. Maybe she would see him at Madame Bayonne's. But only Madame Bayonne sat on the porch. She was wearing eyeglasses and reading a book. Madame Bayonne looked at her a long time each time she went by the house. She must have known what had happened.

Friday she went to the store twice, but he was not there; neither did she see him on the porch. She drove through the quarters on Saturday. She saw only Madame Bayonne. Madame Bayonne was sitting on the porch basing a chair with corn shuck.

Again Madame Bayonne looked at her a long time
each time she went by. (She did not know whether
Jackson had told Madame Bayonne, but she knew
that Madame Bayonne knew. That old woman
knew everything. Some of the children used to call
her a witch, but that was not it. Madame Bayonne
knew human beings.) She went back to the house.
She stood at her bedroom window, she stood at the
kitchen window, she sat out on the front porch, she
walked across the yard under the big old moss-
laden trees—but he never did go by. He must have
left. She wished there was some way she could find
out—some way. But how? Ask someone? Ask
whom? She knew how the people felt about her.
Before Jackson came there, only a few of them
would speak to her. Now, none of them did. Whom
could she go to, whom could she ask? Brother? Yes,
why not try him. He was Jackson's friend.

She drove to Three Stars that evening and
knocked on the back door. The Negro who came to
the door, dressed all in white, including a big white
cap, told her that Brother was not there. Could he
help her? No, he could not. She got into the car and
drove away. She looked for Jackson again when she
went past the house. Nothing. She felt as though she
would die.

She wanted only to see him—that was all—only
to see him. She did not want anything else to
happen. She did not want him to touch her, she did
not want him to kiss her—she wanted only to see
him. From a distance, from near, only a glimpse,
and that would be enough. But, no—nothing.

Catherine was standing at the kitchen window when she thought she saw Jackson going down the quarters. The man wore a green shirt and brown pants, and he was walking with his hands in his pockets and his head down. Catherine watched him go past the little gate, then the big gate, and her heart sank in her body, because it was not Jackson.

She went back to her ironing board in the center of the room. She tried to forget Jackson and think about the dance that she was going to that night. She wondered what the girls would be wearing at the dance. The dance was informal, so they could wear almost anything. She wondered what her cousin Jeanette would be wearing. She was glad that she was going to see Jeanette. She had not seen Jeanette in a long time.

CHAPTER FORTY

Catherine sat at the kitchen table, looking through one of the magazines that Lillian had brought from New Orleans. She had dressed for the dance and now she was waiting for Raoul to come home so they could eat and then leave for Bayonne. Della sat across the table from her with Nelson in her arms. Nelson was wide awake, but he sat as quietly as if he were asleep. He had been like this ever since he saw his mother dressed to go out. In her room down the hall, Lillian was still getting ready for the dance. She had started before Catherine, but she could not find the proper combination of hat, shoes, and dress to wear.

"Better go and see 'bout her," Della said.

"She'll make out all right."

A moment later they heard Lillian coming down the hall toward the kitchen.

"Cathy, see what you can do with this zip."

Catherine started to lay the magazine on the table, but she picked it up again.

"Let Mama help you," she said. "I don't want to lose the place I'm reading."

Lillian looked quickly at Catherine. She probably would have gone back up the hall if Della had not already pushed Nelson away and been standing up to help her. She turned her back to Della, and Della began working with the zipper. Catherine looked up from her magazine at them.

"Getting it?" she asked Della.

"Not yet."

The zipper had caught in the seam of the dress and could go up only a few inches. Della drew it back down a couple of times and pulled it up again, but each time it stopped in the same place. She drew it all the way down, and Catherine noticed her working with the seam. She could see the side of Lillian's face, too, and Lillian looked as though she was becoming more irritable by the second. Catherine looked at Della as Della drew the zipper up again. It moved much more freely this time, and Catherine could see that Della had worked it loose from the seam. But just as she passed the original

"Somebody is," Catherine said. "As soon as you take your bath and eat."

"Bath?" Raoul said.

"That's right," Catherine said. "A bath."

"Didn't I take one of them things last week?" Raoul said.

"I don't know about last week," Catherine said. "But you're taking one tonight if you're going with me."

"And if I don't?" Raoul said.

Catherine was silent. She knew Raoul could and would change his mind with little provocation. An hour later they were driving out of the yard.

CHAPTER FORTY-ONE

Raoul was so deep in thought when Catherine stopped the car at the only red light in Bayonne that he had to look out at the theater to reassure himself that they had already gotten there. He had not moved from the place he had sat in when he first got into the car. He had sat against the door directly behind Catherine, and he had not even shifted his feet.

Raoul wore a blue striped double-breasted suit. His green necktie seemed almost as wide as the lapel of his coat. With the brim of his gray felt hat broken down over his eyes, Raoul was the perfect picture of the gangster made famous by Hollywood during the thirties and forties.

While sitting in the backseat of the car, Raoul had been looking at his two daughters. First, Catherine. He liked the way she combed her hair—the pride she took in showing its full length. He could imagine the two little pearl earrings and the string of beads around her neck. At the house he had wanted to tell her how lovely she looked, but he had not said anything. If he had said anything to her, then he would have had to say something to Lillian, also. Another reason he did not say anything was that he felt he had no business going to Bayonne tonight when he had to get up before daybreak in the morning to go out into the field. "That priest" wasn't going to take five cents of "that money" to pay anybody to come back there and help him, no matter how far behind he got in his work.

Raoul looked at Lillian. Lillian sat back in the seat, staring out in front of the car as though she were in a deep trance. Raoul looked at the little white hat sitting up on top of her head, and at her hair twisted into a big ball in back. He could also see one of the small earrings and the pearl necklace that he had given her several Christmases ago. He supposed it was the same necklace, since he could not imagine where she could get another one from. He knew that in spite of those high and mighty words those in the city used, they would not put out money for anything.

Raoul shook his head and looked out of the window.

"Something the matter?" Catherine said. She had

been watching him through the rearview mirror.

Raoul shook his head.

Lillian looked halfway around, but did not look at him, and looked out in front again. The light turned green and Catherine drove off. After she had gone two blocks up the street, she made a left turn down a dark road that led back of town.

I don't know what happened, Raoul was thinking. I don't know. It was a mistake to put her there in the first place. I told her mon that, but . . . he tried not to think about it any more. He knew he had it all wrong. He knew that it was not Della who had put her there, but that it was his people who had insisted that she go with them when they were sure . . . but he did not want to think about that either.

He had his Catherine; and that was enough. He looked at her again. He looked at her beautiful brown-black hair and the natural way it curled at the ends. He loved the way she handled the car, and he knew if he closed his eyes for an hour, for a day, he was in safe hands.

Something caused Raoul to turn his head to the left, and he noticed the weeds along the ditch bank. Damn, he thought. They call this a town and they got more weeds here than I got in my cane field. He thought about his field again; he thought about all the time he would lose tomorrow just because he came here tonight.

Catherine stopped the car in front of her aunt's house, and passed Raoul the keys. A young woman standing on the porch, wearing a red dress and white shoes, watched them come into the flower garden.

"Hello, there, you old sweet," she said, coming up to Catherine and kissing her. "Hello, there, old Lily. You're just like a living doll." She kissed Lillian. "And hello, there, old Uncle." She kissed Raoul. "Ah, I'm so happy you all finally got here. Was getting ready to say you all weren't coming. What happened? Car broke down?"

"I had to feed my mules," Raoul said. "You don't mind?"

"Oh, gruff to you," Jeanette said to Raoul. "Gruff, gruff."

They went inside the house, and three women met them in the living room. Margaret Toussaint, Jeanette's mother, a little heavier than either of the other two women, and who was to be chaperon that night, smiled at her two nieces when they came into the room. Elvira Carmier, whose name was once Wills but was changed back to the family name two years later because that " 'Merican nigger drank everything that poured," went up to both girls, hugged them and kissed them on the jaw. The third woman, who was called Bertha Taveras, wearing a light-blue dress and a large red flower pinned just over the heart, was not a relative; but she had been trying to get into the family now for a long time. She looked at the two girls and smiled, and then she looked at Raoul who stood near the door as though being around so many women talking at the same time made him feel uncomfortable.

"How's everybody been?" Catherine asked.

"Suffering," Elvira said. "This heat's been murder the last few days."

"I came from work today, and I tell you I could do nothing but sweat," Jeanette said. "Been drinking beer ever since, and it hasn't done one ounce of good. I think it did worse."

"Why don't you all sit down?" Elvira said. "You all going now?"

"I think we ought to," Jeanette said. "Maybe Cathy and Lily will want something cold before going inside. That hall is so hot."

"I thought Maggie was taking y'all," Raoul said.

"Oh, gruff to you," Jeanette said. "Gruff, gruff."

"Maybe we ought to go now," Margaret said. "I don't mind having a Coke or something myself. Will you all mind, Cathy? Lily?"

"A Coke would be nice," Catherine said. "It is a little warm."

"Good," Jeanette said. "Off to the dance, to the dance. Ahh, I'm going to dance and dance and dance—cha-cha-cha."

"Catherine," Raoul said, nodding toward the kitchen. Catherine followed him. "I want you and Lillian back here no later than twelve o'clock, you hear?"

Catherine nodded her head.

"And that cousin of yours there, she drinks. If she starts that tonight—"

"You don't have to worry about me, Daddy."

"I'm not," he said. He wanted to smile to show her that he had confidence in her, but he did not.

"You got enough money?"

Catherine nodded. "I have enough."

"Your sister?"

"I think so."

Raoul took out his wallet and gave Catherine another dollar.

"For the Cokes," he said.

He put the wallet back and took out his watch—a big gold watch with a gold chain and gold numbers on the dial. His father had given him the watch on his twenty-first birthday. The watch had been passed down from father to son for the past three generations. But there was no one for him to pass it to.

"Eight thirty now," he said. "By twelve."

He put the watch back in his pocket, but he was not through yet, and Catherine knew it. The rest of what he had to say was not said out loud. It was said with only a look, but Catherine understood it as well as if he had spoken each word. *Since you're going to the dance, I guess you'll have to dance with them, but as soon as the dance is over, you go over there and stand where Margaret is standing, and make Lillian do the same. And, listen, I don't care what reason you might have, I don't want you or Lillian going out of that hall unless Margaret is there with you. Do you understand?*

Catherine understood, and they went back into the living room. Jeanette was dancing a waltz in the center of the floor; when she saw her uncle she danced toward him and barked again.

"Ready?" Margaret asked.

"Ready," Catherine said.

Jeanette danced toward Elvira who stood at the mantelpiece.

"Good-bye, Aunt Vy," she said.

"Jeanette, you're only going to the dance," Elvira said.

"I don't know," Jeanette said, dancing toward Bertha Taveras. "I might dance all the way to California, hot as it is. Good-bye, Madame Taveras. It's been so good knowing you."

"Good-bye, Jeanette," Bertha Taveras said, and started laughing. Bertha Taveras was one of those big, sensitive women who could laugh or cry with little provocation.

Jeanette danced across the room to Raoul who stood against his sister's sewing machine.

"Gruff to you," she said. "Gruff, gruff to you."

And she turned and danced toward the door, followed by her mother and her two cousins.

"Cards?" Elvira said. "Why don't you hang your hat up, Raoul?"

"Yes; cards," Bertha said. "Hand me your hat, Raoul."

She took the hat and left the room, but a moment later she was back. Elvira had already set up a small card table in the center of the floor, and while Bertha placed three chairs around it, Elvira got a deck of cards, a notebook, and a pencil out of a drawer. She put the things on the table, took her seat, and began shuffling the cards.

"How's the work?" Bertha asked Raoul.

"Hard," Raoul said indifferently.

"Unbutton your coat," Bertha said. "You'll burn up."

"Better yet, take it off," Elvira said.

Raoul did neither. He cut the cards and Elvira started dealing them out. After the second hand, he unbuttoned the coat, but still kept it on.

"How are the folks?" Elvira asked.

Raoul knew she was talking about their mother and their aunt, and not about Della. Della did not exist as far as she was concerned.

"All right," he said, taking a card off the deck, and then laying one out of his hand down on the table.

"Aunt Rose's garden?"

"All right, I suppose," Raoul said. "I ain't seen it since I plowed it up."

"Gin," Bertha said.

Raoul and Elvira counted what they had on the table, subtracted what they had in their hands, and Raoul gathered the cards and started shuffling them again.

"Why didn't you bring me a melon?" Bertha asked. "You know how much I like them little sweet country melons?"

Raoul pretended he did not hear her. The two women looked at each other, and Elvira said, "He never think about people in town."

"That's the true, Raoul?" Bertha asked.

Raoul did not answer. He cut the deck in halves and shuffled the cards again.

"Is that the true, Raoul?"

He cut the cards, shuffled them again, and set the deck in front of Bertha.

"Cut," he said.

"You never think of people in town?" she asked.

Raoul pushed the deck toward his sister.

"You want cut?" he asked her.

"Look at me when I talk, Raoul," Bertha said.

"Cut," Raoul told Elvira.

"I'm getting me some water," Elvira said.

"Sit down," Raoul told her.

"I can get some water if I want," she said.

"Sit down," Raoul told her.

"Look at me, Raoul," Bertha said. Raoul turned to her. "Say you love her, Raoul. Say it in front of your sister; in front of God. Say you love her."

Raoul continued looking at her, but did not say anything.

"You don't love her. You never loved her. And all I want to do is make you happy. That's all."

"I thought one dick in this heat would be enough," he said.

"Is that a nice thing to say, Raoul?" Elvira said. "And in front of me, your own sister?"

"He just want to make me cry," Bertha said. "Make me ruin my face. All right, I will cry and ruin my face. If that's what you want, I will cry and ruin my face."

She stood up from the chair, and already the tears had come into her eyes.

"Can I go lay 'cross your bed a while?" she asked Elvira.

"Of course, honey," Elvira said.

Bertha looked at Raoul again before leaving the room. She would have forgotten what he had said if he had only looked up at her.

"Oh, Raoul, Raoul," Elvira said. "Why do you have to say that to her? All she want you to do is look at her sometimes. Talk to her sometimes. Is that asking too much?"

"You cutting?" Raoul said.

"Cut yourself," Elvira said. "You act like a damned priest—forgive me, Father in Heaven. Now, you got me swearing." She looked at Raoul. "Raoul," she said. "Catherine is not the answer."

"You ain't cutting these cards?"

"I'm not cutting any damned cards."

"Then shut up," he said.

"I'm not shutting up," Elvira said, getting up more courage. "This is my house, and I talk in it as much as I want. No, she's not the answer. She's not. And no matter how much you love her, she can't take the place of a woman."

Raoul began shuffling the cards all over again. He would play a game of solitary.

"Raoul, let her go. Let her go, Raoul."

But he was not listening any more.

"Let her go, Raoul," Elvira said. "Give her a chance. Give her a chance before it's too late."

He began laying out the hand of solitary, and Elvira knew there was no use talking to him any more. She stood up from the table and looked down at him a moment; then she went into the bedroom where the other woman was.

Raoul took out his watch to look at the time. It

was only nine o'clock. That meant he had three more hours to stay here—even more if they did not come back at midnight as he had told them. He put his watch back.

If there was someplace else he could go, he would have stood up that moment and left. But there was not another place in Bayonne. He would not go near that dance hall, and not one of the bars in Bayonne was fit for a man to drink in. And since he did not visit anyone else here—Baton Rouge, New Orleans, or any place else for that matter—he had no alternative but to sit where he was and wait. Maybe later he would go for a walk, but he was not sure that he would do even that.

CHAPTER FORTY-TWO

Jackson bought his ticket at the door and went into the dance hall. The hall was packed and very hot. The three big fans in the ceiling were spinning at full speed, but they were not doing very much good. Women and girls who were not dancing sat in chairs along the wall fanning themselves with pocket handkerchiefs and cardboard fans. The music was fast and wild, and there was dancing everywhere.

After standing at the door a moment, Jackson moved farther into the hall. He looked for Catherine, but he did not see her. He started toward a window, but the window was crowded with people laughing and talking. He moved along the hall toward another window, but this one was crowded also. He stood there a ·moment looking for Catherine, and then as he started to move again, he felt someone touch him on the arm. He turned around; it was Lillian.

"See you made it?"

"Yes."

"Got my letter?"

"I got it yesterday."

"I'm glad you could make it. I'm sure she'll be glad to see you. She missed you. She missed you very much."

Lillian said all of this very fast—too fast for Jackson, as a matter of fact. It sounded to Jackson as though she had been rehearsing the lines. He looked at her. What was in it for her? Why had she written the letter? And why was she saying this now? He remembered how she had looked at him from the window that night he and Catherine had the argument in the yard. She had not blamed him at all for what he did—for the way he cursed Catherine and threw her back against the tree. On the contrary, she seemed to be blaming Catherine for not leaving with him.

"Do you love her, Jackson? Do you?"

"I love her, Lillian."

She smiled—a forced smile—one that was not necessary. Her eyes were on Jackson, but she seemed to be looking at something far away. Jackson did not like Lillian. There was something evil about her. There was something deep and evil in her that he did not like. He turned away and looked out on the floor again. The people were dancing in front of him and to either side. He looked for Catherine everywhere, but he did not see her.

Then after he and Lillian had been standing there a few minutes, he saw Catherine coming toward him. She was looking very pretty and happy. She was with another fellow—a tall mulatto, quite handsome, and dressed in an Ivy League suit. The mulatto's hand was on Catherine's shoulder. Jackson's face and neck began to burn him; he felt himself breaking out into a sweat. He saw Catherine stop. She had not known he was there. She had not seen him before now. Then he saw her start toward him again. The mulatto never did move his hand. They came over and Catherine spoke. She seemed both awkward and frightened.

"Paul Aguillard; Jackson Bradley," she said.

The mulatto, smiling, stepped forward and shook his hand; then he moved back and put his hand on Catherine's shoulder again. Jackson's face burned even more; his heart began to race in him. He wanted to jerk the mulatto's hand away, and he wanted to hit Catherine with his fist. Nobody's hand should be on her but his own.

"I went over where you were sitting, but Aunt Maggie said you'd come this way," Catherine said to Lillian.

"I saw Jackson come in," Lillian said. "I came over where he was."

Catherine looked at Lillian a long moment as

though she did not know what to do next. Then she turned to Jackson again. She tried to seem composed. She even raised her head a little higher to show how at ease she was.

"Thought you had gone back?" she said. She was so at ease now that she could even smile when she said it.

"I'm still here," he said cuttingly.

She did not know what to say, but she had to say something.

"Enjoying yourself?"

"Are you, Catherine?"

She looked at him a moment before answering. "It's all right."

They did not say any more, but they continued looking at each other. *He means nothing to me*, Catherine said with her eyes. *He means nothing to me*.

Jackson looked at the mulatto. The mulatto was quite handsome. He wore very nice, expensive clothes. He looked quite intelligent. He would probably end up teaching in a college or maybe he would become a lawyer. He seemed like the professional type. And maybe that was what she deserved, Jackson thought. He would give her much more than I ever could. He could give her a nice home, security; what could I ever give to anyone? Should I walk out of here now, this moment? But where will I go, and what to? He turned to Catherine again. Her eyes had never left his face.

"So that's where everybody is," Jackson heard someone saying behind him. It was Jeanette who was coming over to where they were. "Oh, hello there," she said to Jackson. "Yes, I must say, you are boss. Yes, I like that." She whistled and smiled coquettishly at him. "Got me looking all over the place, and everybody is over here," she said to the others. "Hello, Paul, you're still with us? Thought you'd left by now?"

"I'm still here, Jeanette," the mulatto said in a French accent, which he obviously liked very much.

"Yes, I see," Jeanette said. "I see. Yes, indeed."

There was silence after this. Even Jeanette was silent. Everyone except Lillian was feeling uncomfortable. She liked what was going on. She had noticed how Catherine and Jackson had looked at each other. She knew they wanted to be with each other, and eventually they would be. And, too, she did not like this fellow Paul. She did not like the Ivy League clothes that he wore to impress people; she did not like his French accent; in short, she did not like him at all.

After a while, Paul's hand slipped away from Catherine's shoulder. He did not know why, but for the first time that night he thought his hand was out of place.

"Well, well, well," Jeanette said. That was all for a while. Then she said, "Say, Paulie, baby, how would you like to give me a spin?"

"I have a partner, Jeanette," Paul said.

"Ahh, come on, give a helpless little old Creole gal a break—huh, Paulie, baby, sweetheart, dumpling?"

Paul looked at Jeanette the way you might look at a bad child that you better not turn your back on. He whispered something to Catherine, and he and Jeanette went out on the floor. Jeanette looked back at the others and winked her eye, then she and Paul started dancing. Both were very good dancers.

"I'm going back," Lillian said, walking away.

Catherine and Jackson were alone. There was a moment of silence between them.

"It's awful warm, isn't it?" Catherine said.

"Yes, it is."

They were silent again. He was looking at her, but she pretended to be interested in the dancers out on the floor.

"Would you like some fresh air?" he asked her.

"That would be nice," she said.

CHAPTER FORTY-THREE

When they were outside, they went across the yard toward the church. Many more people had come out of the hall, and they were standing in the yard under the trees, talking and smoking. Catherine and Jackson moved through the crowd toward the back of the church.

"How has it been?" she asked him.

She had said it in the way she might have said it to a stranger that she was meeting in the street. It did not sound right to her, and not at all to Jackson. He did not answer her.

Catherine turned to him to see why he had not answered, and he pulled her closer and kissed her very hard on the mouth. She had wanted him to do this, and yet, for a moment, she fought against it before yielding to him.

"Why the other night, Catherine?"

"Where can it go?"

"Where do you want it to go?"

"You know I love you."

"Do you?"

"Do you have to even ask?"

"Yes."

She could not believe he meant it, and she moved away from him. There was a bench under one of the trees, and she went to the bench to sit down. He sat beside her.

"If you only knew what I've gone through this week," she said. "We both know how impossible . . ." She looked at him questioningly, even with hope. And at the same time, she knew what his answer would be.

"Why is it so impossible?"

"Could you ever come back here?"

"No, but you could leave."

"Leave?" she said, as though the word awakened something in her.

He nodded. "Leave."

She had thought about leaving. She had thought about leaving with him when she heard he was going back. But remembering them at home, she realized how insane the whole idea was.

"Why didn't you go? I thought you had gone. Why didn't you go?"

"You wish I had gone?"

"Yes."

"No, you don't, Catherine."

She turned her head away. Her shoulders began trembling, and she brought her hand up to her face.

"It would have been better. It would have been better." She looked at him again; she was crying. "I don't like what you're doing to me, Jackson. Don't you see what you're doing to me?"

"I love you. You don't want me to love you?"

"You're tormenting me."

She stood up. He stood up with her. She touched at her eyes with a small pocket handkerchief and composed herself again.

"I have work to do," she said. "This is my place. My work is here."

"Your heart is with me. Mine is with you, Catherine."

"Who can follow his heart the way time is?"

"I can."

She looked at him. "Can you? No, you can't."

"If I were to stay, is that it?"

"Yes . . . if you were to stay."

"You know that's impossible. You know I can't put up with this any more."

"I know that," she said hopelessly. "I knew it all the time. I was dreaming."

"Is that why we quit seeing each other?"

"That's part of it," she said. She was leaning back against the church, looking far away. She looked at him again. "If you knew how much I wanted you . . . how much I wanted to go back to that room in Baton Rouge . . ." She looked away again.

"What's to keep us apart, Catherine?"

"We must think about the others. We must think about them. We owe them our lives."

"How about our own lives? Yours and mine?"

"My life?"

"Yes."

"I'll get snatches of happiness where I can," she said, looking far away.

"Like with this guy Paul?"

"He's a good dancer. That's all."

"Is that part of your plan?"

"I love to dance."

"And can you be satisfied with that?"

"No. But there will be other little things."

"And will these other little things satisfy you?"

"I hope so."

"We both know differently, don't we, Catherine? We both know we need each other, don't we? You want to leave that place, and you know it. And I need you, and you and I both know that."

She turned her head. He turned her back to him.

"All of our lives, we've loved each other. All of our lives. Isn't that so? Isn't that so, Catherine?"

She did not answer him.

"Isn't that so, Catherine?"

"They have nothing," she said, trying to make him understand. "They have nothing. Do you know what it means to have nothing? Nothing?"

"I know. I know."

She shook her head. "You don't know. You have no idea."

"I know," he said. "I know what it means to have nothing. To not believe—" He stopped. He was not supposed to say this. He could tell by her face that he was not supposed to say this. With her you must believe—you must definitely believe in something. She looked away. They were silent. He looked at her long and hopelessly, but she continued to look away. "Maybe you're right," he said. "Maybe you're right. What do I have to offer you? Paul has much more, hasn't he? I have nothing. I have nothing in the world—"

She put her hand on his mouth to make him stop. He held her hand with both of his and kissed it.

"You love me, don't you? Don't you?"

She was afraid to say it.

"Don't you?"

She was afraid to say it now.

"Come with me, Catherine," he said. "Come with me. You want to go, don't you? You want to go, don't you?"

Yes, yes, yes, was in her heart. But she would not say it now. She could not say it. What about the others? But he saw it in her face.

"Come, Catherine. Come."

"No," she said, shaking her head, angrily.

"Come," he said. He had grasped her arm now, and he was pulling her away from the church. "Come."

"No," she said desperately. She was trying to hold onto the church now. "No."

"Come," he said, pulling on her.

"Please," she said. She was not angry now, she was frightened. "Please, please," she said.

But he would not stop pulling her.

CHAPTER FORTY-FOUR

Raoul stood on the porch and watched the two men come up the street. He had been standing out there about ten minutes, trying to decide where to go. He did not know where to go, but he was tired of sitting inside. He watched the two men cross the street just as they were coming up to the yard. He thought he saw one of them looking toward the house, but he must have been imagining this. What would they want here? Who could they be coming here to see? The men came up even with the car and stopped, then one of them came up to the gate. The other man followed only a moment later.

"Raoul?" the first one called to him.

He did not move; he did not answer. He recognized the two men now—they were from Grover; but what could they possibly want with him? He had not spoken to them, neither had they spoken to him, a dozen times since he had been living there.

"See you?" the man said.

He hesitated again. What did they want? Borrow money? That was impossible. Maybe something had happened at the dance. Maybe something had happened to Catherine. He went down the steps. He could see the two men standing close together as though they needed each other for courage.

"Henry," he said. He looked at the other man, but he did not speak to him.

"Just thought you might want to know something," Henry said.

Raoul looked at him, waiting. He did not know whether he would believe him, whatever he had to say.

"Catherine fooling around up there," Henry said.

Raoul stared at him, not showing belief or disbelief. He knew these people hated him. He knew they would do anything to hurt him. But he would not let them see how he felt.

"Just thought I would tell you," Henry said. "She up there right now behind that church. With Charlotte boy."

Raoul stared at the man on the other side of the gate. Suddenly his face became very hot, burning him. He tried not to show anything, but the men could tell that he was angry.

"Just thought I would let you know," Henry said. He nodded, and he and the other man walked away.

The two Negroes had been approached only a

couple of days ago by two of the Cajuns who farmed the plantation. The Cajuns had promised the Negroes twenty dollars each if they would let Raoul know that Catherine and Jackson were seeing each other. The Cajuns had given the Negroes ten dollars apiece then, and had promised to give them the rest of the money after Raoul caught Jackson and Catherine together.

The two men had seen Catherine and Jackson come out of the dance hall and go to the back of the church. They stood under a tall cottonwood tree between the church and the dance hall looking at them. They had stood there a long time smoking, and trying to make up their minds whether they should tell Raoul or not. They did not want to tell Raoul, but now that they had taken the Cajuns's money, they were afraid what might happen to them if they did not.

"That's where he at?" one asked.

"Course," the other said. "Where else he go'n go? One sister or the other."

They had seen Margaret Toussaint come to the dance with the girls, so they knew Raoul must be at Elvira's house. They had said very little to each other all the way up to the house, and now as they went back, they did not say anything to each other at all. They separated the first chance they got.

Raoul stood at the gate unable to move. He knew they hated him. He knew they would do anything to hurt him. Maybe they were saying that only to make him do something foolish. Charlotte's boy? Charlotte's boy? She did not have a boy, did she?

No, her niece had a boy. They had gone to California long ago. Was that the boy he saw at the store the other day? He thought he looked strange. Was that him? And now that he thought about it, he felt at the moment that the boy was looking at him differently from the way the others were. But was he only imagining this now? He might have been. The boy might not have been at the store at all.

He wondered if they were telling him the truth. Maybe they were doing it only to make him angry. Why did they come to tell him? Why didn't they just laugh at him behind his back? They did not tell him about the other one. (He thought about the other one. It was like a haunting song that stays in one's mind. It had been in his mind twenty years. Even after the death of the boy ten years ago, it would not leave. It seemed to grow stronger. Time seemed to feed it.)

Raoul looked up the street. The dance hall was at least a half mile from where he was standing, but he looked in that direction anyhow.

Why were they doing this to him? Why? What was in it for them? He continued to look up there. He did not believe them. Catherine would never . . . he knew she was lonely. Of course she was lonely. A girl at that age . . . He had been noticing something different about her the last few days. She had been going around the house as though she were drugged—half of the time not hearing, half of the time not seeing. . . . No, no, no, he was wrong. He was imagining this, because those niggers had told him that about her. He did not believe them. They were doing this to hurt him. The Cajuns were probably behind it all. They wanted his land. He knew it. They would do anything to hurt him, to make him pack up and leave. They would . . . he wondered if she would do this to him.

"Raoul?" Elvira called from the door. He did not answer. He had not heard her. "Raoul," Elvira said, "who was that?"

He heard her, but he did not answer her this time either. He opened the gate and went toward the car.

"Raoul?"

He was in the car now. He pressed the silver button on the dashdrawer, and the door popped open. He worked his hand around in the drawer until he found the revolver, then he took it out and stuck it under his belt.

"Raoul?" Elvira said, running toward the car. "Raoul?"

He pulled away just before she got there. He went up the street, turned the corner, and headed back.

He drove along slowly. He was not trying to think. He was not trying not to think. Things simply ran through his mind. She will be there. She will be dancing. She will be dancing with someone her own color. . . . She will be standing by Margaret. Margaret will be sitting in a chair fanning. . . . She will be outside. He will have his black arms around her waist. He will have his black mouth on her red lips. . . . I will raise the gun. I will—he started thinking about the other boy. It was like a song that you could not get out of your mind. It was like your skin that you must live inside of forever. (Contrary to what the others believed, he loved the boy. Ten thousand times he had wanted to pull the boy to him, to hold him against his chest, to cry, to whisper, "I love you, I love you"; but something always kept him from doing so. How could he explain what it was? He did not know what it was. It was there with him all the time. "Hate him," the thing was saying to him. "Look what she's done. Hate him. Look what she's done. Hate him. Hate him." And all the time he wanted to love the boy. He wanted to pass his hand over his skin, over his hair. He wanted to feel the small bones in his hands and arms.)

A car horn blew in front of Raoul. The damned fool was coming straight toward him. No, he was headed toward the other car. He pulled to the side, almost running into the ditch. He was there. Already he was there. He must have driven a little faster than he thought. He did not know what had happened between the time he got into the car and now. He could not remember stopping at any corner, seeing anything or anyone.

He parked the car and started walking. All of this seemed strange to him. A magnet seemed to be drawing him, and he was not moving by his own power. He could have been walking on foreign soil; he could have been around people who spoke a different language. If he were in his field now, if he were a million miles away from here now . . .

He started to go inside the dance hall, but stopped. He went across the yard. The people moved out of his way. He was not walking faster than anyone else; his face did not show anything. But the people felt his desperation and moved out of the way.

He went around the church, but he did not see anything. He almost stopped and looked under the church—but would he lower himself to believe such a thing? Did he think she would lower herself? He would kill those two men if they had lied about her. He would kill both of them with his bare hands.

He went back across the yard. The man at the door told him he would have to buy a ticket if he wanted to come in. He did not say anything. He only stared at the man. The man tried to stare back at him, but saw it was no use.

"Be sure to come right out," the man said. The man wanted him to know he was letting him go in out of the kindness of his heart.

He did not say anything to the man—not even a nod. He went inside. It was like walking into hell for him. Noise and motion everywhere he turned. He began looking for her, but did not recognize anyone. He moved against the wall, looking. Nothing but motion and noise.

A girl with a very red mouth and wearing a very tight dress stood in front of him. He did not say anything to the girl; he had not even seen her. She moved in front of him again. He still did not notice her. She turned to him and smiled, but she must have seen in his face what the people outside had felt meeting him, and she turned and moved away. He continued looking for Catherine.

"Well, I'll be—" Jeanette said. "What—what are you doing here? The next dance mine?"

Jeanette looked as though she had been drinking. She was giggling uncontrollably.

"Where is she?"

"Who? A special one—Uncle, no?"

He looked at her, and he could not control how he felt. His face showed everything now.

"Where's your mon?"

Jeanette grinned. "Over there. The world must be coming to an end."

He looked at her and turned away. He found Margaret and Lillian sitting on chairs against the wall. When they saw him, both of them looked as though they had seen a ghost.

"Where is she?"

Margaret could not say anything for a while. She stared at Raoul with her mouth open.

"Where is she?" he asked.

"Who?"

He did not say any more. He looked at Lillian. Lillian looked back at him fully for several seconds, then she turned away. She tried to hold back what she felt, but it was as plain on her face as his feeling was on his. As she turned her head, he thought he saw a little smile come on her mouth.

"I see," he said to Margaret. "I see."

"Out there dancing," Margaret said. "Where else?"

He nodded. "I see."

Then something snapped in him. They had gone. She had left him. He whirled.

"Raoul?" he heard Margaret calling. "Raoul?"

He ran out of the place—out of noise, motion, odors—into the fresh air. Margaret was behind him, and he ran harder. "Raoul? Raoul?" Something else snapped in him. She would have to go home first. She would have to get her things—the child.

CHAPTER FORTY-FIVE

She had no control over anything any more— neither her mind, nor her heart. Ideas came into her mind, but went out just as fast. She caught glimpses of trees, houses, lights from an automobile, the river, but the next moment all of it had slipped by. She sat there as though she were paralyzed—not being able to think properly, nor being able to move. I will not see Bayonne again, I will not see the trees again, I will not see the river again, I will not see him, my father, again, I will not see Lillian again, I will not see Jeanette again, I will not see the church again, I will see none of what I'm seeing now again. . . . I will be happy. I will not be happy. I will love him, I will love my child, I will make a decent home for him and my child. . . . No, I will not be happy. To be happy, one must work and believe. He does not believe. No, he won't be happy, and I won't be happy either. You must work, work, work; that is the only thing. That is the only way to be happy. Our life does not belong to us. Our life belong to them. No, our life belong to us. To live and to love, that is life. I love them. No, I love him. I love them, yes, I love them. Before he came I loved them. No, I've always loved him, and I always will. . . . What will he think if I tell him it is not right to go—that they will have nothing? Can he understand they are not like other people? Lily knows that they are not like other people, that's why Lily must go. That's why I must stay. I must stay, Jackson. I must stay. Darling, don't—I love you so much, darling. I . . . the trees go by, the houses go by, the cars, the fences, the river, Louisiana—my life.

"What are you thinking?"

Silence.

"Catherine?"

"Nothing."

"Please tell me."

"Nothing."

He looked at her a long moment—inquiringly; then he looked out at the road again.

"I'll make it up to you," he said. "I swear I will. I will love you. I will love you with all my heart. It will be just us. It will be just us always."

Us? us? us? and nobody else but us? Is that what you want? Oh, Jackson, that is not life. Oh, Jackson, darling, can't you see? Us? How long can it be like that? How long? Can't you see that's what happened between them? Can't you see there must be others—something else in our lives, can't you see?

"I'll take you home. Then I'll go back and get my suitcase. Then I'll come back and get you."

She was silent.

"Catherine?"

"Yes."

He began slowing up the car to turn off the highway. Will she ever see this again? The Grovers' big house? the store? the cypress trees? the river-bank? the river? Will she ever see it black and lonely like this again? They were in the quarters now—the black, old deserted quarters. How could she love—she was not trying to think about this; it slipped into her mind just as everything else did.

"I'll see you in about ten minutes," he said. He had stopped the car before the door. She did not move. "Catherine?"

She turned to him, looking at him as though he were someone she had never seen before.

"Ten minutes," he said.

She did not answer, she did not even nod her head, she got out of the car and went into the yard. There was a light on in the front room. Of course Della would be up waiting for them to come back. Any other time she probably would have been in bed long ago. Della unlatched the door as she came up on the porch.

"Where's Raoul and Lillian?" Della asked.

She went past Della into the room. Della jerked her around.

"What happened?"

"I'm leaving."

It did not sound right. It did not sound right at all. If she had said she was going into her room to hang herself, it would have sounded much more natural.

"You doing what?"

"I'm going with him."

"You out your mind? You know what you saying? With who? Jackson?"

"I'm leaving with him."

She was not looking at Della, she was looking over her. She talked as one might talk in his sleep.

"You ain't leaving this house," Della said, taking her by the arm.

"Get him ready for me. I have to pack."

"Did you hear me?" Della said.

She pulled her arm free, and went down the hall to her bedroom.

"Catherine," Della said, following her. "Not me. Don't think about me. I can go on. I can go on like I always did—by myself. But he can't. He can't. You hear me?"

She did not answer. She got the suitcase from on top of the chifforobe and laid it open on the bed. Della moved out of her way as she came back to the chifforobe to get her clothes.

"Get Nelson ready, Mama."

"You think I'm go'n join you in this?"

"I'll do it myself."

After putting as many clothes as she could in the suitcase, she locked it and put it by the door. Then she got another suitcase from under the bed and began packing the rest of the clothes in it. She was not throwing the things into the suitcase, neither was she taking so much time to fold them neatly. She was doing everything carefully, as she always did everything.

"I'll need some money."

"You think I'll give you a penny?"

She did not say anything. She did not look at her. She went across the hall to get the baby. Nelson was asleep. When Catherine sat him on the bed to put on his clothes, he became half awake. He rubbed his eyes with his fist and looked at her. After she had put on his clothes, she put on his cap, and then let him lie down again. He went back to sleep.

She went to the chifforobe to get her hat. She stood before the mirror putting it on. Then she opened the small door of the chifforobe and took out a wallet. She counted the money in the wallet and put the wallet into her purse. She came back to the bed and sat down.

"I knowed you would be his death," Della said. "I knowed that from the start."

Catherine did not say anything. She did not even look at her. Her hands were clasped together, and she stared down at the floor as though she were completely alone. Maybe this was all a dream. Maybe none of this was happening. How could it possibly be happening?

She heard Jackson coming up on the porch. Della went to the front to open the door for him, and a moment later they were back. They were both looking at her, but she would not raise her head. She did not believe that this was happening to her. This could not be happening to her.

"Catherine?"

She looked at him. It was not a dream; it was real. She picked up the baby and let her eyes go toward the suitcases. Jackson came forward to get them.

She turned to Della. But she did not know what to say. Nothing would have sounded right. She went out of the room. When she pushed open the door to go onto the porch, Raoul was standing there with the gun in his hand.

CHAPTER FORTY-SIX

"Catherine, you leaving?"

"Let us by, Raoul," Jackson said.

Raoul had left his coat and hat in the car and his shirt was soaking wet with sweat. He had not heard Jackson; he did not even see him standing there. He could only look at Catherine with disbelief.

"You leaving?" he said again. "You leaving?"

"Get out of the way, Raoul," Jackson said.

"Catherine?" Raoul said.

Jackson made a step toward the door; Raoul turned the gun on him.

"Boy, I don't want any more blood on my hand," he said. "I don't want any more gnawing at my heart. Don't make me use this—please."

"Then get out of the way and let us pass."

"Catherine?" he said to her again. "Didn't I do all I could?"

Jackson could see that Catherine had begun listening to what Raoul was saying, and he pushed her toward the porch.

"Get your hands off her," Raoul screamed at Jackson. The gun was shaking in his hand, and Raoul was doing all he could to keep from pulling the trigger. "Get your hands off her. Get away from her."

Jackson moved quickly now and knocked Raoul's hand to the side. The gun fell, and when Raoul tried to pick it up, Jackson kicked it off the porch into the yard.

"Get to the car," he said to Catherine.

"No," Raoul said, coming on him. "You not taking her from here. I'll fight you like a dog. I'll fight you till I'm dead."

"Get to the car, I told you," Jackson said to Catherine.

She got between them instead.

"Daddy," she said. "Daddy, please."

"I'll die first," Raoul said, knocking her to the side.

Catherine fell against the wall and then on the floor. The baby started crying in her arms. Jackson went toward her, but he saw Raoul coming on him. He threw the suitcases to the side and jerked off his coat.

"That's my father," Catherine screamed at him. "For God's sake—no."

Jackson jumped to the ground, and Raoul came

on the ground after him, swinging his arms wild and frantically. One of his fists caught Jackson on the shoulder, and Jackson fell back against the porch. Raoul sprang at him, and Jackson moved to the side. Raoul slammed against the end of the porch, was stunned for a moment, and turned on Jackson again. Catherine gave the baby to Della and ran down the steps to get between them. She screamed at one, she hit the other; she pulled on Jackson, and pushed on Raoul. But neither one heard her or felt the little blows she gave him on his back or shoulders. However, she felt the blow Raoul gave her in the side. Raoul had not meant to hit her; he was swinging at Jackson when she got in the way. Jackson saw her fall and try to get up, then she went back down holding her side. He continued backing away from Raoul, and Raoul continued moving toward him. He paid no attention to where he stepped. Any direction Jackson moved, he followed. His fists shook with impatience to hit him.

He ran at Jackson and swung and missed. But he spun around and swung again. This time he hit him a solid blow on the shoulder, and Jackson fell down on the ground. Raoul kicked at him once, then twice, but Jackson rolled away each time. Raoul moved in to kick at him again, and this time Jackson knocked Raoul's legs from under him.

They got up at the same time, standing toe to toe, pounding each other with both fists. Jackson hit Raoul in the face, and blood shot from his mouth. He hit him again, cutting him under the eye. But this did not stop Raoul a moment. He swung both of his arms like someone crazy. If he missed with one, he swung the other. When Jackson moved to the side, he spun around and swung again.

Catherine got between them with a piece of wood, hitting one then the other, but not hitting either one hard enough to hurt him. She probably would have done as much good if she had stood ten feet away and told them to stop.

Jackson hit Raoul every time Raoul got close to him, but this did not stop Raoul at all. Blood dripped from his mouth and from the cut under his eye, but he paid no attention to his wounds. Nothing mattered to him but Jackson. If Jackson moved right, he was there. If he moved left, Raoul was there, too. Most of the punches that he swung at Jackson missed, but the ones that connected hurt him every time.

Jackson knew Raoul was trying to back him into the porch, but he could not get away from him. Then when Raoul was close enough, he broke on Jackson with his arms spread open. Jackson hit him dead in the chest, but this did not keep Raoul from throwing his arms around his waist.

Jackson could smell the sweat on Raoul, and he felt Raoul's sweaty and bloody face brush against his shoulder when Raoul threw his arms around him. He felt Raoul's arms getting tighter around him, and he tried to break himself free. But Raoul's arms were like a vise around his waist. His wrists were as hard as knots in a tree. Jackson put his hand under Raoul's chin and tried to break himself free, but Raoul rolled his head to the side, and Jackson's hand slipped away. He tried again to pull Raoul's arms from around his waist, but this effort was as futile as the one before. He felt all of his blood rushing up to his head. He thought he heard Catherine screaming at them and hitting Raoul, but he was not sure. He felt himself going, and he knew he would pass out if he did not get himself free. He managed to spin Raoul around and hit his back against the end of the porch. He drew back and hit hard again. He felt Raoul trying to swing him around, but he would not let himself be manhandled. He drew back and hit again and again. Then he was loose.

He felt dizzy as he backed away from the porch, but he kept his eyes on Raoul. Raoul knelt on the ground with his hands pressed to his side. He saw Jackson standing there, and he started crawling toward him. Jackson backed away. Raoul got to his feet. Jackson let him make one step toward him, then he swung and caught Raoul fully in the jaw. Raoul went down. He got back on his knees and looked at Jackson. He was breathing hard, and Jackson thought he saw tears running from his eyes. Catherine knelt beside him, but he pushed her away. It was not violent, he had done it with only a slight movement of his hand. Catherine came to Jackson. If Raoul would not listen, maybe he would. She did not say it—she pleaded with her eyes. Jackson held her away and watched Raoul get to his feet. Raoul came on him with both fists clenched and shaking. Jackson hit him before he had time to swing, and he fell again. He lay silently a moment, then he got back on his knees. He was definitely crying now—softly, but definitely. Both Catherine and Jackson could see him crying.

Catherine went to Raoul and put her arm around his shoulders. But Raoul was unaware that she was even there. His eyes were on Jackson, who stood before him. He did not look at him angrily. Instead, he seemed puzzled. He tried to grasp what was happening to him. He would not believe that he was beaten. There was too much left for him to do. There was the crop to get in; there was Catherine. How could he possibly fall? What would become of everything if he did?

Raoul tried to get up, but he went back on his knees. He did not believe that his strength had failed him. He believed deep inside of him that he had not tried hard enough. He pushed himself away from the ground and got to his feet. He felt tired and weak, but he made himself go toward Jackson anyhow. He swung, Jackson moved his head only an inch, and Raoul fell to the ground. For a moment, there was only silence. Then Jackson heard a sound, a sound that could have been made by man or animal, but which was definitely a sound of defeat.

Catherine helped Raoul to his feet, and Jackson watched them go toward the house together. When they came up to the steps, Raoul told Catherine he had to sit down. Catherine sat beside him and passed her hand over his face. Raoul would not raise his head.

CHAPTER FORTY-SEVEN

Della had been standing in the door all the time watching the fight. Nelson started crying again, and she held him closer. But she had not said anything to him—not even a whisper—and she had made no attempt to stop the fight in the yard. The fight had been coming a long time, and as long as it was between just the two of them, she did not care who won or lost. Now as she moved toward one of the chairs against the wall, she looked at Raoul and Catherine sitting on the steps. She remembered what Raoul had said in the door about the blood on his hand.

So he did kill Marky, she was thinking. She nodded her head. So he did kill him. And all these years, I thought it was an accident. So that's why he wanted her there—to soothe the wound, Raoul? to stop the gnawing? Oh, Raoul, Raoul—how you must have suffered all these years. And I thought I was suffering. Oh, my poor, poor husband; my poor, poor man.

Jackson had not moved. He stood in the yard looking at Raoul and Catherine on the steps. His whole body was aching. The knuckles on both of his hands were skinned. He was still breathing hard. He felt something running down his face and he raised his hand to wipe it away. He did not look at the blood on his hand—he was still looking at Raoul and Catherine. He went to the steps where they were.

"Catherine?" he said.

Catherine raised her head a little and looked down again.

"Catherine?" Jackson said.

She did not answer, neither did she look at him. Beside her, Raoul raised his hand and wiped the blood from his mouth.

"I was wrong," Jackson said. "I was wrong. But he made me fight him."

Catherine did not answer. She sat forward on the steps with her head bowed. Raoul raised his hand to his face to wipe away the blood again.

"Don't you see that's why he did it, Catherine, to make you stay? It's pity he wants. That's all it is. Pity."

Jackson noticed the quick jerkings of Catherine's shoulders, and he knelt in front of her and took her face in his hand.

"Catherine?"

She looked at him. The tears ran down her face.

"He made me fight him, Catherine," Jackson said. "I didn't want to fight him. I ran. I ran and ran from him. But he made me fight him, because he wanted this to happen."

Catherine looked at Jackson, and the tears continued to run down her face.

"I love you, Catherine," Jackson said. "I love

you, sweet. Do you think I'd do anything to hurt you? He kept after me. He kept after me, Catherine . . ."

She shook her head and looked down again. Jackson started to touch her, but drew back his hand. He looked at her a moment and turned to Raoul. Raoul leaned forward on the steps with his chin almost touching his chest. Now that Jackson had knelt by the steps, he did not raise his hand to his face any more.

"Why, Raoul?" Jackson said. "Why are you doing this to us?" Raoul was silent. "We love each other, Raoul. We love each other. She loves me, I love her."

"Go with him," Raoul said, with his head down. "It's over with."

Catherine turned to Raoul and put her hand on his arm.

"It's not over with, Daddy," she pleaded. "It's not over with."

Raoul was silent. The blood dripped from his face to the steps, but he did not raise his hand any more. Catherine wiped his face for him.

"It's not over with, Daddy. You have stood this long. You can keep on standing. I'll stand beside you."

"You been the prop long enough."

"I don't mind being the prop, Daddy. I love my daddy. I don't mind being the prop."

Raoul glanced at her half-heartedly, but he would not look in her face.

"It's not over with, Daddy," Catherine said, trying

to encourage him. "It's not over with."

"Catherine?" Jackson said.

"You have stood a long time, Daddy. I won't ever let you down. I'll—"

"Catherine?" Jackson said, jerking at her.

She turned to him. She was crying hysterically now. She had forgotten that Jackson was still there.

"I can't leave him now. . . . I love you with all my heart. . . . But I can't leave him now. . . . Can't you see? Can't you see?"

"How about Mrs. Della, Catherine?"

She cried harder. Jackson took her face in his hand, and she threw her arms around him. Jackson held her closer, kissing the side of her face and her hair passionately. Raoul sat on the steps with his head bowed. He did not look at them once.

"Have faith in me," she cried. "Have faith in me." She drew herself away and looked at him. "I will come . . . Not now. But I will come. I swear. I swear."

"Catherine. . . ?"

"Just have faith in me," she said, pleading with her eyes. "Just have faith in me."

She turned to Raoul again. She laid her arm across his broad, bent shoulders, but Raoul did not seem to be aware of her.

"Daddy?" she said. "Daddy?"

He turned toward her a little, as though he was hearing his name called from a great distance away, but he would not look into her face.

"Come, Daddy," she said. "Let's go inside. "Let

me look after you, Daddy."

She put one of his arms over her shoulder and her arm around his waist. "Come on, Daddy," she said. "Come on, Daddy."

"Catherine," Jackson said, standing up with them, and taking her by the arm. "This is not your job, Catherine."

"Yes," she said, nodding her head. "Now more than ever. But it won't be for long. And then I'll come."

"How will I live till then?"

"You must . . . and I will. Then we'll be together."

He watched them go up the steps, then inside the house. He felt as though part of his life had slipped away from him. His throat got tighter and his eyes were burning. For a long time he stood there looking at the darkness inside the room.

Jackson looked at Della sitting against the wall with the baby pressed to her bosom. It was dark on the porch, but he knew Della was looking at him, and had been looking at him all the time that he had been standing there. He got his coat from the end of the porch and started to walk away, but he stopped and looked at her again.

"You leaving without saying good-bye to me, Jackson?"

He went up on the porch and stood before her with his head bowed.

"Be patient with her, Jackson. I waited more than twenty years for this night."

He did not understand what she meant. She could

tell he did not, and she stood up and looked at him. He was cut just above the right cheek, and she touched the bruise with her hand.

"Come in and let me look after that," she said.

"I'm all right."

"Then I better go in and look after my husband," she said. She looked at Jackson and nodded her head. "Yes, he needs me now. This the first time in twenty years I can say that: 'Raoul needs me.' " She smiled thoughtfully. "You don't understand? It's easy to understand. This the first time he ever fell in front of her. All his life he lived for two things, her and that field out there. She stayed here for him, and he had to be hero enough for her. But now he's fell. You the hero now, Jackson."

He did not say anything. He felt like anything else but a hero.

"No, you right, you not a hero. But he's a proud man, and after what happened tonight, he won't ever be able to raise his head in front of her like he done before. So that means she'll have to leave. He'll see to that. And then I get my chance—a chance I been waiting for for twenty years. No, I'm not proud to see my man get beaten. No woman wants that. But what happened here tonight is the best for everybody. If y'all hadn't fought out there, and if he hadn't got beaten, he wouldn't 'a' never let her go."

"She hasn't gone yet."

"She'll go. He'll see to that. And I'll make her come to you. Not a reward for what you did, Jackson. If you was anybody else, you wouldn't 'a' lived to walk out of this yard. But you Jackson. Marky. You been Marky ever since he—since he died. He died by accident, you understand what I'm saying?"

"Yes, ma'am."

"Out there tonight, my husband and Marky was fighting. Whose side I was supposed to take? No side . . . not after living like this all this time. No, tonight it had to be settled. Tonight it was settled." She looked at him and nodded her head thoughtfully. "Now, I must go in and look after my husband," she said with pride. "Will you excuse me, please."

She went as far as to the door, then she stopped to look at him again.

"You wait for her, you hear? If it takes twenty years, you wait."

He watched her go into the house. He stood there, hoping that Catherine would come back outside. But she never did.